Forbidden Affair

C. L. Conolly

FORBIDDEN AFFAIR

Copyright © 2012 by C. L. Conolly
Cover and author photo by Julie Witt Photography

C. L. Conolly
clconolly@gmail.com
Cypress, Texas

ISBN-13: 978-0-9886876-0-8

Printed in the United States of America

10 9 8 7 6 5 4 3 2 1

To my parents, Mike and Sylvia Merola,
for having faith in my dream.
And to my husband, Karl Conolly,
for answering all my disturbing questions about weapons
and encouraging me to continue to ask.

Forbidden Affair

One

The last thing I remember about my mother was when I was six. On a normal day, she would drop me off with a neighbor and leave me until it was my bed time.

I was excited that day because it was the first day that I could remember her taking me with her. She took me to a fancy hotel. Other than the look of fear on her face, I thought of the trip as a vacation.

We walked through the front doors and directly to the elevator. She pressed the call button and we waited.

I looked up at her and smiled, but she never took her eyes off the doors. When the tone sounded to signal it had arrived, we stepped in. She pressed the button for the top floor. Without a single word, she stepped out of the elevator and glared at me as the doors closed between us. That was the last time I saw her.

I remember thinking, maybe she is playing hide and seek and I was supposed to find her. I went all the way to the top floor of the hotel, the doors opened and a gentleman got on. He looked down at me and I sat in the back corner of the elevator.

The man pressed the button for the lobby and I pulled my knees up to my chest. He looked back down at me.

"Are you lost?" He asked.

"No. My mother and I are playing hide and seek. She sent me to the top to give her time to hide so when I got back down I could go find her." At that time, when I said it out loud I didn't even believe my own words.

When the elevator stopped at the lobby, the doors opened and the man put his hand over the door to hold it open.

"I hope you find her. Good luck," he said, helping me to my feet and giving me the chance to exit the elevator first.

I smiled at him and began wandering around the lobby, peeking behind chairs and under tables. I knew in the back of my mind I was never going to find her.

I was found by a desk clerk - I'm sure hours had gone by - huddled between two chairs in the lobby. I had been crying and all I wanted was to go home.

My life technically began at fifteen when I met my two best friends Charlotte and Jillian. We lived together in a group home. The three of us were orphans.

By the time I had met Charlotte and Jillian, I was in my twentieth group home. They were straight A students unlike my D's. Our foster parent's said they only rewarded good behavior. Charlotte was a typical teenage girl who was rewarded with a cell phone and the ability to date.

Jillian concentrated on her classes but also had a cell phone. I had no social life outside of Charlotte and Jillian and they were all I needed. Sure, I was a little jealous when Charlotte would go out with her boyfriend, but I did always have Jillian.

I do remember one group home I was in around the age of twelve. When I lived there, I always tried to get straight A's in order to impress one particular boy, Jojo. I loved him and I knew he cared about me, but nothing ever came of our relationship.

When I turned thirteen and he was fifteen, he was adopted by an older couple who wanted to help teen orphans in order to make sure they became functioning members of society rather than taking up space in the corrections facilities.

Once he was gone, I purposely became a problem child hoping, maybe even wishing, I would be adopted by the same couple just so I could see him again. All that got me was a few more foster homes before making a permanent stop with Jillian and Charlotte.

After high school graduation, the three of us went to Europe for a month. We saved for three years to take that trip.

One day for lunch, we went to a small café in London. Charlotte saw an extremely handsome man from across the room. Giggling she whispered, "That is the man I am going to marry."

"Charlotte, you don't even know him. He could be one of those crazy European guys who kidnap female tourists and sell them into prostitution," I warned her.

"Oh, Mackenzie. You worry too much," Charlotte told me.

"Don't you ever watch 20/20? Barbara Walters reports all the time about American women who travel to Europe and are never seen again. When they are found, they are part of some kind of perverted old man sex slave group."

"I haven't even talked to him yet. Can I at least meet him before you label him as a perverted old man sex slave group leader?" She asked giggling.

"Fine, but if he asks you to come back to his hotel room with him, we're leaving," I told her, wagging my finger in her face.

Fortunately, he was American. He also was on a graduation trip to Europe. He and Charlotte were married within a year. Sure, I resented him for a while for taking away one of my best friends. Eventually I accepted, Tom Moore.

Jillian and I bought a house together, until the day she found Mark Geary. They were married within ten months.

I now felt alone, again. I was back to my suffering in silence phase. I was, in my mind abandoned, again. I stayed in the house and Jillian and Mark purchased a new home.

Charlotte and Jillian had come up with a way to keep us together. Every Wednesday we had lunch together and every Friday night the five of us went out to dinner.

During one of our lunches together, Charlotte decided I needed to find someone to fill the void in my life. Her words, not mine.

"I'm fine. We have it perfect. Lunch on Wednesdays, dinner on Fridays. What more could I want?" I told her with a fake smile on my face.

"Kenzie, you know that isn't true. You always need convincing to come out to dinner with us. You're always complaining that you're the fifth wheel and how it will be uncomfortable. You have a chance, right now, to choose the best looking single guy in the restaurant and be happy."

"Hello, ladies. How are we doing today?" Malachi, the manager of the diner, came over to the table.

He was always dressed as though he had just stepped out of the seventies. His suits were a revolting brown color and his ties were striped dark green and burnt orange. He was so creepy and always touched me on the shoulder when he talked to us.

"We are doing just fine, thank you. How's the food industry treating you?" I asked trying to make polite conversation.

"Well, you know with every business there are busy days and slow days." Luckily, our food arrived just then. "Enjoy your meals ladies."

He lingered behind me for a little while placing a hand on each of my shoulders before inhaling deeply as though he smelled my hair then walking away.

I shivered as soon as he was out of sight. "He gives me the creeps," I said just before shoving a bite of food into my gob.

"I think he has a crush on you," Charlotte said smiling.

"That is disgusting. I would rather be alone."

"Well, maybe if he thinks you're taken he will leave you alone. Look around the room and find you a winner."

"Charlotte, my life doesn't work that way. Just because you and Jilly found husbands that way doesn't mean I will. I'm not as pretty as you two are. No one could fall in love with me like Tom did with you and Mark with you, Jillian." I pressed the heels of my hands into my eyes and rubbed.

"Mackenzie, you are just as beautiful as we are. Guys don't flock to you like they have to us because of your confidence. You have to feel confident, look confident and play hard to get. When he looks at you and smiles, you smile back, with a confident smile. Give him a look with your eyes that says, 'come here' then look away." Jillian continued rambling advice as I scanned the room with my eyes.

An extremely handsome man, with dark hair and eyes, was glaring at me from across the room. I kept my eyes locked on his. He smiled. Trying my confident smile, I smiled back. He sort of giggled then mouthed, *Hi.* I wiggled my fingers at him in a sort of wave, which made him giggle again. Apparently, my awkwardness flattered him.

He stood up and headed my way. A slap on my arm broke my gaze. "Owe, what?" I looked at both of them, who were smiling at me like a couple of teenage girls.

"Shh, he's coming. Look." Charlotte nodded in his direction.

"Hello, I'm Jasper Tulley." He extended his hand.

I smiled awkwardly at him again and shook his hand. I didn't know what to say so I just giggled.

"She is Mackenzie Leigh and I am Charlotte Moore. That is Jillian Geary." Charlotte took Jaspers hand from mine but our eyes stayed locked on each other.

Finally, I looked down at the table and he acknowledged her and Jillian. "How are you ladies, this fine afternoon?"

"We're all doing well, thank you," Jillian responded.

"Would you like to have dinner with me tonight, Mackenzie Leigh?" His voice was soft, not quite a whisper but calming.

I couldn't say anything, but I did nod.

His eyes were green, but they had small flecks of brown in them. They were hypnotic and I couldn't look away. He looked familiar in a very refreshing way. I couldn't put my finger on it, but I felt as though I knew him from somewhere.

"I'll see you then. Eight 'o clock, at the corner." He ran his forefinger over the back of my hand still keeping eye contact. He turned and walked away.

I watched him walk out the door and through the parking lot to a beautiful light blue with silver sparkles Mercedes sports car. There was something about him that seemed mysterious and I was determined to find out what that was.

"See Mackenzie, you can meet a man." Charlotte smiled at me.

"I think I know him from somewhere. He looks oddly familiar," I voiced.

"Don't ruin this just because you think you know him from somewhere and assume it is somewhere bad," Jillian told me.

"I never said it was from anywhere bad, I just said he looks familiar. Almost like maybe I went to school with him."

"Whatever, he was cute. I say give it a try," Charlotte said.

"I will give him a chance and meet him for dinner. If he turns out like Malachi, then I'll ditch him," I said smiling.

We all laughed and turned our attention to the diner manager who was sitting a few tables away.

Two

For dinner Jasper took me to a small quaint bistro. He ordered soup for our appetizers and a couple of cold cut sandwiches for our meal. For what seemed like twenty minutes, all we did was stare into each other's eyes. I was first to break the silence, "What do you do, Jasper Tulley?"

"Do for what, Mackenzie Leigh?"

"Work silly." Our eyes never parted.

"I'm an investor. What do you do?"

"I'm a writer. I have a small column I write for the local newspaper." The server brought over our soup and we continued to make small talk.

"That sounds like an interesting job. What do you write about?" He asked before spooning a sip of soup into his mouth.

"It is just a small column about activities everyone can enjoy on any budget," I explained.

"Is it just local or anywhere in the continental United States?"

"It is pretty much all over the world. I give myself a particular budget, then every once in a while I go on a little mini vacation to find out if I can survive on the money I have or if I have to pull out more while I'm there." My soup was now lukewarm so I was able to eat it fairly quickly.

"Sounds like fun. How did you land that kind of a job?" Jasper asked. He lifted the soup bowl to his lips and guzzled down what was left.

His eyes were so beautiful. They were familiar to me, in a way, comforting. Even his face was beautiful. Words could not explain how I felt about him. There was an odd tingling sensation that surged through my entire body every time his skin encountered mine.

There was an instant connection. I had only just met him a few short hours ago and I was already dreading the end of the night.

Our soup bowls were replaced with our entrées. We ate in silence. When the plates were cleared and the check paid, Jasper touched my hand and said, "You are the most beautiful woman I have ever met. Please promise me I can see you again."

My body tingled. "How about Friday night? My friends and I, with their husbands, all go out to dinner. You could be my date and even up the odds," I giggled.

He chuckled, "I would love to. But do I have to wait that long before I see you again?" He actually had a sad look in his eyes.

I smiled, flattered. "How about a walk, tomorrow afternoon. I know the best little ice cream shop just down the street. I will meet you there at two."

We stood up to leave. He held open the door for me and held my hand as he walked me to my car. The tingling sensation returned which caused me to shiver. We gazed into each other's eyes again. I wanted him to kiss me. Desperately, I wanted him to kiss me, but he didn't.

He extended his hand, "Until tomorrow."

"Until tomorrow." I was confused as I shook his hand. I didn't know if he was really that into me or if he was just putting on an act.

There was something about him that I wanted to know more about. A strange connection I felt pulling me toward him as though I had known him somewhere else in my life.

Hopefully Charlotte and Jillian would ask him the questions I wanted answered since whenever I looked at him my brain turned to Jell-O. My feelings for Jasper Tully were unlike anything I had ever experienced-except when I was with Jojo.

* * *

Thursday afternoon was short. I met him outside the ice cream shop. I already had an ice cream cone in my hand and was licking the melting drops that were racing down the cone. As he approached, his face seemed to light up when he spotted me.

"What is it about you that makes me so happy?" He asked as he extended his hand to me again.

I wasn't sure why he wouldn't hug me or touch me any other place but my hands. It was really beginning to confuse me. I just shrugged my shoulders. I couldn't smile. I didn't understand him. He didn't make sense to me. Did he have intimacy issues? What was he thinking? Maybe he is married and is afraid someone might see us and tell his wife.

"What are you thinking about?" He asked me as though he could read my thoughts, but wanted me to say it out loud.

"Why is it that you only shake my hand every time we have contact?" I noticed the look on his face must have reflected the expression on mine.

"I'm sorry, it is just that you are so beautiful that whenever I see you I don't know how else to act. I just want you to see me as a gentlemen and not one of those jerks that just grabs women and treats them like possessions rather than people." I saw his cheeks change pigmentation as the rosy color appeared.

I was, of course, smiling. His comment made me feel special. *He* made me feel special. Only one person ever made me feel this way, but I knew I would never see him again. I didn't know how to react.

The only thing I could do was flee. "Well, I'll see you tomorrow night," I said as I turned, threw my ice cream cone in the trash and darted toward my car. I left Jasper standing there with a confused look on his face.

On my way back to my house, I stopped off at Charlotte's place. I sat in my car for a few moments before getting out to knock on the door.

"Mackenzie, what are you doing here?" Charlotte asked when she opened the door.

"Can I come in?"

"Sure," she said as she stepped aside to give me room. "What brings you here?"

"I just saw Jasper again."

"That's a good thing, right?"

"Well, there is one thing that really irks me about him." I gave her a rundown about his behavior.

Charlotte listened intently. Once I finished, she said, "what do you want me to do?"

"I don't know what to do. There is no way he can be this interested in me this fast. I just met him yesterday. How can anyone like someone so much so fast? The only thing I can think to do is run," I rambled.

"Mackenzie, slow down. We will have dinner with him tomorrow night and Jillian and I will let you know what we think of him. Then you do what you want with our advice. Is that okay with you?" Charlotte rubbed my back as we sat on her sofa.

I breathed slowly then replied, "Okay, I think I can handle that. How did you know that Tom was the one?"

"The way he complimented me, the way he made me feel and the way his face would light up every time he saw me." She smiled as she reminisced. "How does Jasper make you feel?"

"When he talks, well as he talks, he makes me happy. After he has said it and I have time to think about what he has said, I wonder how he knows I'm as wonderful as he says I am and what his intentions really are. He speaks as though he knows me, personally. Every time he touches me, my whole body tingles and begs for more. It's as though my body wants his body pressed up against it." I ran my fingers through my hair and breathed deeply as I imagined what it would be like to have his body against mine.

"Kenzie really, wait until Jillian and I give you our opinion of him before you run away. I know this is the first man that has given you attention without an ulterior motive."

"The only question I really want to know the answer to is why he will only shake my hand?" I immediately realized my feelings for Jasper were stronger then I anticipated for someone that I had just met when tears streamed down my face. I told her, his explanation to me when I confronted him.

"Maybe he's married." Charlotte giggled which only made the tears fall faster. "I'm sorry Kenzie. I didn't realize you really did like him that much. You have always lectured Jillian and me that love at first sight does not exist. You have only known Jasper for a short time and now you are contradicting your own thoughts."

"I know, I know. My heart wants to get close to him but my mind tells me to run far away as fast as I can. What do I do?" I reached for a tissue from the center of Charlotte's coffee table and swiped the leakage from my nose.

"Jillian and I will grill him at dinner tomorrow night and find out what his intentions are. Can you wait until then?"

"Thanks Char. I will go home, work and try to get him off my mind." We hugged, then she watched me walk out to my BMW convertible.

I went home and attempted to work on my articles, but all I could think about was Jasper. His eyes, how they mesmerized me and had me in a trance every time I looked into them. I always seem to lose my mind in them. The strange way his green eyes seemed to have a hint of brown in them.

I also couldn't stop thinking about the way that I really wanted to see him again. His beautiful face, the broadness of his shoulders and how strong he must be. Oh, how I wanted him to hold me in those arms. Jasper was the only thing on my mind. I just couldn't figure out what was so familiar about him.

Since I couldn't work, I just decided to go to bed. I turned on the news and dozed off.

* * *

That night I dreamt of Jasper Tulley. His mid-length brown hair was flowing in the wind as he drove toward me in his convertible. I was standing outside my house in what appeared to be an exquisite dress manufactured sometime in the mid-twenties. He was dressed in a tuxedo.

He stopped the car in front of me and leaned over to open the door for me. I couldn't take my eyes off him as I lowered myself into the passenger seat. He touched my hand and the tingling returned.

The force when he sped off closed the door. We didn't speak until he stopped.

"Where are we?" I asked.

"I'm going to take you somewhere no one will find us."
The look in his eyes was soft yet frightening.

We walked down a dirt road to an eerie old shack that
appeared as though it were manufactured of old fence
wood. "I don't like this place. Can we go back now Jasper?
I want to go home."

"Not quite yet. I want to show you something." There
was no emotion in his voice.

He led me inside and motioned for me to sit down on
what appeared to be an old barber's chair.

He rolled a metal surgical tray over in front of me.
There was a cloth over top, which he yanked away as
though it were some sort of magic trick. Apparently, my
expression was amusing because he began to laugh. Now I
was terrified and began to tremble.

"What is going on Jasper? What are you doing? What
are you planning to do?"

"Shut up and stop asking so many questions. I can't
concentrate with you talking so much."

He picked up a scalpel and examined the blade. He
turned it back and forth in his hand scoping out both sides.
He lifted it up over his head and before I had a moment to
react, he plunged it into my abdomen.

I screamed in pain. I thought about how he had made
me feel the other times we had been together. He was so
sweet but secretive. He was caring but confusing. I could
feel the blood pouring out of my body. Just before I passed
out, I woke up screaming.

The bed was soaked with sweat. I was soaked with
sweat.

I glanced over at the clock as I reached for my phone,
realizing that if I were to call either Jillian or Charlotte at

this hour, they would chew my head off, literally. I replaced my phone on the bedside table.

I reached for the television remote and pressed the power button. I decided to take a shower and forget about my dream.

Charlotte would tell me it's just my subconscious trying to find fault in a perfect man for me. He has never treated me any way but good and I have been trying to find a reason to push him away. I just let it go and hoped for a perfect evening.

I spent most of the day going back and forth between writing my article and choosing my outfit for dinner. We weren't scheduled to meet until seven thirty, so at three in the afternoon I decided to just go out and buy a new outfit.

I stopped at about twenty different department stores. Once I was satisfied with what I had chosen it was already seven fifteen. I was going to be late to dinner. I made the purchase then rushed out to my car. Speeding, and looking around for cops, I managed to make it to the restaurant just in time, but I still needed to change my clothes.

I took the bag inside with me and slipped off to the restroom without being noticed. I quickly changed, stuffed the clothes I had taken off into the bag and attempted to fix my hair as best I could with what I had. I stepped out of the lavatory, nonchalant and stepped up to the table where my friends were.

"Sorry I'm late, but the traffic was horrible," I lied as I greeted all of them with a hug.

"Are you sure you didn't just lose track of time while shopping for that fabulous new outfit?" Jillian questioned as she cut the tag off the blouse I was wearing.

Embarrassed, I just shrugged and smiled. "Has Jasper arrived yet or are we still waiting on him?" I looked around the place hoping to see him walking up.

"I'm sorry hun, he hasn't arrived yet." Tom rubbed my arm with a look of concern in his eyes.

"Let's give him until eight then we will order." I continued to look around for the next half hour, glaring at the front door waiting for him to cross the threshold.

When he didn't show by eight, I thought I could feel my heart breaking. I pouted for the rest of the night. I didn't understand why it was when we first met he couldn't wait to see me and now he has decided to stand me up. I continued the night with my friends and decided to forget about my three-day crush.

Three

For the next week, I just went through the motions of my life wondering where I went wrong. Monday I turned in my columns for the week after.

I could hear my editor, Colleen, speaking, but I was inside my head, thinking, not listening to a single word. I wasn't even really sure if she was speaking to me, or just thinking out loud.

"Mackenzie, is there something on your mind? You seem distant today," my editor said across the table in the conference room.

"I'm okay, Colleen. My mind is just not all here right now. I'm sorry; I'm back. What were you saying?"

"I was just saying that these five articles lack the passion your articles usually have. The beginning of the week is strong, but from Wednesday, they just seem amateur."

"I'm sorry. I've had a lot going on these last few days. I guess I just haven't been focused. Give me back the ones you feel need work and I will have them to you tomorrow in tip top condition." I put out my hand and faked a smile for her benefit.

Colleen handed me three articles with a puzzled look on her face. "Are you sure you're okay? You can talk to me, you know. I won't judge you."

"I'm okay. I just need to focus my frustration into my work. I will take these home and tweak them to bring them up to standard." I smiled at her again, this time genuine.

I left the conference room with my head held high attempting to exude a newfound confidence, when in actuality I was wondering what was wrong with me. I never allowed anyone to come between my work and me, ever. I was going to push Jasper out of my mind and write three phenomenal articles the paper has ever seen in hopes to regain the professional standard Colleen has always seen from me.

On my drive home, just to see, I took a detour and drove down the street the diner was located. There, out front, was his car. Parked and waiting for him to return. I couldn't believe it; he was at the diner again. *How dare him.* I thought. *How dare he show up at the exact diner he knows I frequent with my friends. What is he doing here? What does he want?*

I parked my car and stepped out. I couldn't move. Now that I was outside the car, I didn't really know what I was going to do, or say. I thought about the articles I needed to rewrite. I turned to get back into my car.

"Mackenzie! Mackenzie Leigh!" A familiar voice yelled from behind me.

I turned slowly to see Jasper coming toward me. I froze. I didn't want to talk to him. Just the thought of looking into his beautiful eyes would have me hooked again. He smiled and waved as he befell closer and closer to me. Panicking, I retreated to my car and pulled away quickly before I was sucked into his charming demeanor once again.

I watched in the rear view mirror, as Jasper stood in the middle of the parking lot, stunned. I went straight home to work and forget that the last week ever happened.

* * *

Tuesday, I returned to the newspaper. I handed the revised articles to Colleen who nodded in approval as she read.

"These are you, Mackenzie. This is what I am used to seeing from you." Colleen placed the articles down on the table then looked up at me, concerned. "Do you want to talk?"

"About what?" I asked. I pretended nothing was wrong even though I still thought about Jasper more than I wanted to.

"Are you sure you're okay? You know you can talk to me about anything. I'm not only your boss; I'm also your friend. Please feel free to confide in me whenever you need. You can always call or stop by anytime. You are welcome here even when you aren't just turning in your articles." Colleen stood and came around to stand next to me.

"Colleen, trust me. I'm just fine." I patted her shoulder, flashed my fake smile, turned and left.

I drove straight home this time instead of passing by the diner. I couldn't handle the heartbreak if I saw Jasper again. I decided to read a few fan letters before beginning my articles due the next week.

* * *

Wednesday, I did my usual household chores. Laundry, sweeping and mopping floors, cleaning bathrooms, vacuuming, and that was all before lunch.

I met my friends at our usual lunch spot. Charlotte and Jillian were already there waiting for me. Jean, our regular server, was standing behind the host podium.

"Hiya there, Mackenzie. I got somethin' for ya," her thick country accent pushed the words out of her mouth. She handed me an envelope with my name glued across the front letter by letter as though they were cut out of a magazine.

"Where did this come from? Who gave this to you?" I held the envelope by the corner as though it were covered in sludge.

"I dun no. It was dropped off Monday. I got Monday's off. Malachi says some guy came in, said for it to be given to you on Wednesday. I came in yesterday and he gave it to me sayin' it was for my Wednesday regular, so I held on to it."

"Thank you, Jean." I sauntered over to the same table we sat at every week. I was still holding the envelope as though it were infected with anthrax.

"Hey, Kenzie," Jillian said as she stood to embrace me.

"What's that?" Charlotte asked.

"It was dropped off here for me on Monday. Jean gave it to me when I got here. I saw Jasper here that day. I wonder if it's from him." I held it up for them to see.

"Are you going to open it?" Jillian sat down and drummed her fingers on the table.

"I don't know if I want to know what he has to say. He stood me up for dinner." I tossed the envelope onto the table and took my seat.

"Just open it and see what it is. Maybe he has an explanation for why he wasn't there Friday night." Charlotte pushed the envelope closer to me with the tips of her fingers.

I stared at it while the two of them tapped in rhythm. I looked up and made eye contact back and forth between the two of them before finally snatching up the envelope and tearing into it, removing the contents.

I couldn't speak. In my hand was a Polaroid photo of a young woman who lay, tied to a bed. She was wearing a baby doll T-shirt that was pulled up exposing her breasts. Her skirt was pulled up and her legs were spread as though she had been raped. Both hands strung up to the headboard, one leg pulled to the footboard and one leg missing. Blood was pooled on the floor, dripping from the bed which had stained the sheets.

She appeared dead. Two words were glued at the bottom of the photo with the same letters as on the front of the envelope.

'Your next,' it read.

"Whoa, what kind of photography is that?" Malachi said from behind me.

"What is it?" Jillian asked her eyes glued on my expression of terror.

When I didn't respond, Charlotte reached across the table and snatched the photo from my hand. "Let us see."

Charlotte and Jillian leaned together to view the photo. Once she saw what it was, Charlotte threw it down on the table and stood up so quickly she almost knocked over a server walking behind her chair with a tray full of drinks.

"Oh my gosh!" Jillian yelled.

Malachi picked the photo up off the table and eyed it as though it were a picture of a woman posing in Playboy magazine. He was focused intently on the Polaroid.

"Wow, I think this girl is dead," he said with such a strange calmness it was as though we were having just a normal conversation about the weather.

"That's beside the point, Malachi. Who would send this to me?" I was fighting back tears. I was determined not to show my fear in case the person who left this photo for me was watching.

"Someone went to a lot of trouble to make sure this one was dead," Malachi snickered.

The tone in his voice made the hair on my arms and the back of my neck stand on end. I stood up and snatched the picture from Malachi's hand. Picking up the envelope off the table I headed for the door.

"Where are you going?" Charlotte asked following me with Jillian in tow.

"To the cops." Once we were outside, I whirled around to face them. "This is the reason you can't trust people you just met. I am planning to have a restraining order written up so I never end up like her." I held the photo up so they could both get a good look at it.

"Who do you think did this?" Charlotte asked.

"The only one person we have just met, Jasper Tully," I said.

"You can't be serious? Mackenzie, do you really think that he came over and introduced himself just so that he could torture you with photos of dead women?" Charlotte said cynically.

"Not with photos, this is a warning. He is going to try to kill me."

"You don't know that. This could have come from any one," Jillian tried to comfort me.

"Who, that we know, would all of a sudden just start sending me pictures of dead women?" I said.

"How many of these pictures have you received?" Charlotte asked concerned.

"Well, this is the first one, but who's to say he won't send me another?"

"Mackenzie!" A familiar male voice shouted. "Mackenzie Leigh!"

I turned and spotted Jasper Tulley jogging toward us. "Don't come near me! You stay away!" I shouted and started to walk away but he took off in a full sprint and before I knew it, he was standing in front of me.

"Is there a problem here?" Malachi appeared in the doorway of the diner.

"No Malachi, everything is fine," I told him.

"Are you sure? You want me to take care of this guy? I could take him out back and beat him to death so he won't bother you anymore," he said.

I didn't think to take him seriously. He said crazy things like that all the time. There was one Wednesday when, for some reason, both Charlotte and Jillian were running late for lunch. Malachi had come over and sat down with me and was saying randomly weird things.

"Have you ever killed anyone?" He'd asked.

"Of course not. What kind of a question is that?" I was baffled by his choice of conversation.

"Have you ever thought about it?"

"I'm thinking about it right now if you don't get away from me with that conversation," I told him just as Charlotte and Jillian had arrived.

I remember feeling relief when he walked away and never said anything to my friends about his questioning. I just blew off the conversation and hoped I was never left alone with him again.

Malachi shot an evil look at Jasper then disappeared into the diner.

"I'm sorry about Friday night. I tried to catch you on Monday to explain what happened but you took off. I didn't realize you were this upset about it," he began to explain.

"Just leave her alone psycho," Jillian told him stepping between us.

"Back off stalker," Charlotte chimed in stepping up between Jillian and Jasper.

"What's going on?" He asked.

"I got the message you sent me. Trust me, no need to explain. This came out loud and clear," I told him.

"What is that?" He extended his hand expecting me to hand it to him.

"You should know. You're the one who sent it to me." I held the envelope and its contents behind my back.

"What are you talking about? I didn't send you anything." The puzzled look on his face made me believe him. I thought I could see the truth in his eyes, his beautiful mesmerizing eyes.

I took a deep breath, calmed down and began to explain my outrage. "I saw you here Monday. Jean said the person who dropped this off for me brought it on Monday. If *you* didn't leave it for me, what were you doing here?"

"I was actually hoping to run into you so I could explain why I didn't show for dinner on Friday." He grabbed my hand.

"Kind of odd seeing as how you know we only come here on Wednesday," Charlotte told him.

"So, start explaining." I pulled my hand back, crossing my arms.

"I had a work emergency," he said plainly.

"That's it? You had a work emergency. That's good to know. Even if there was a slight chance of a relationship, I'm glad I know now that you would BLOW ME OFF FOR WORK!" I tried to walk past him but he grabbed my arm. I yanked it from his grasp. "Don't touch me."

"Please don't be that way. I am here today to have lunch with you now and hope you could forgive me for missing our dinner date. Mackenzie, I'm really sorry. Where are you going?" He asked when I continued to walk past him.

"Come with me. All of you." Jasper, Charlotte and Jillian followed me down the street to the electronics store.

"Seriously Kenzie. What are we doing here?" Jillian asked.

"I am going to do a little detective work of my own. First, I want to know if this girl is on the news and find out if they have any leads." I found the first employee near the televisions. "Excuse me, could you change the channel to a news station please?"

The pimple faced teenage boy rolled his eyes at me before changing the channel. We stood and watched the news anchors droll on and on for half an hour. There wasn't any mention of a homicide or the woman. No missing person report either. I turned, thanked the employee and walked back through the door with the others close behind.

"Where are you going now?" Charlotte asked, sounding irritated.

I turned around and walked backward as I replied, "I am taking this photo to the police and let them know I have been threatened. If they know who this girl is and possibly know who the guy is who did this to her, then maybe they can save me."

"Let's take my car. I have an SUV. We can all fit comfortably." Jillian ushered us to her vehicle.

"I'm still not sure about you, Jasper, so I got shotgun," I said as I stole the front passenger seat. Charlotte slipped into the back with him.

Once we were buckled in, Jillian drove to the police station. Charlotte, Jasper and I passed the picture around attempting to figure out who the girl was.

"I don't know who she is. I don't think I have ever seen her before." Charlotte said as she reluctantly passed the picture to Jasper.

"She does have the same hair color, body shape and the same eyes as you Mackenzie. Her face is different from yours. I don't recognize any of her facial features. I don't know who she is," Jasper said as he passed the photo back to me.

"It's amazing how you can see all that with this poor woman in such a horribly compromising position." I placed the picture face down in my lap.

"Do you think he purposely left her eyes open to make it creepier then it already was?" Charlotte asked.

"I don't know. I'm assuming it wasn't an accident. There is no way he would have left her eyes open if he had any respect for the dead. According to this photograph, this man has no respect for anything, including himself," I retorted. "I have done enough research to know if he were to close her eyes he would have felt remorse."

"If he felt any kind of remorse, he wouldn't have taken the picture," Jasper said.

When Jillian pulled into the parking lot of the police station, I had my seatbelt off and the door open before she had even come to a complete stop.

"I need to speak to a homicide detective," I said as soon as I approached the front desk. The others joined me once they filed out of the car.

"Is there something I can do for you, ma'am?" The lady behind the desk asked.

"Are you a homicide detective?" I asked with a sarcastic tone.

"No ma'am, I'm not. I can forward information to someone for you if you would like." Her rude, polite tone was really beginning to aggravate me.

"Look lady, I need to speak to a homicide detective now before someone else gets hurt." I slammed the photograph down on the desk in front of her.

The look on the policewoman's face was probably the same look I had when I first saw the photo. "Back away from the desk, all of you. Put your hands where I can see them!" She pulled out her gun and aimed it at the four of us.

"Whoa, wait just a minute. I think you misunderstood me," I tried to explain with my hands in the air.

"No talking; face the wall. Put your hands behind your head," the officer commanded.

We complied. Within seconds, eight more police officers surrounded us and began patting us down.

I felt violated as one officer rubbed her hands over every part of my body. She reached in my pockets and pulled them inside out, spilling the contents onto the floor.

We were cuffed and taken over to a desk where they took our jewelry and shoelaces before placing us into a holding cell.

"Good job, Mackenzie. That police lady thought you were threatening her," Charlotte said.

"I wasn't expecting it to turn out like this," I half apologized.

The lights in the cell were dim and the walls were yellowing. Considering the smell of urine which radiated from the small five by five room, I assumed the discoloration on the walls wasn't just from the deterioration of time.

"Now what do we do?" Jillian asked.

"We wait. They will want to question us. When they take us individually into the interrogation room we will just tell them what really happened," I confidently explained.

"Do you think they will believe us?" Charlotte asked.

"As long as we have the same story we should be fine," I said.

"And what story is that oh wise one?" Charlotte mocked.

"Tell them the truth. Exactly how we came into possession of the photo. How hard can that be?" I was sure this was going to be a lot harder to convince them then I was making it sound, but my friends seemed to let out a sigh of relief.

Four

Watching the clock on the wall, I wondered how long they were going to make us wait. It was so high up it was almost touching the ceiling - most likely so the people in the holding cells couldn't change the time or use it as a weapon.

When we were talking, time seemed to fly by, but now - with the silence surrounding us - the clock seemed to have stopped. Since Jasper was being held in a different cell, I wondered what was going through his mind. I speculated he had never been arrested before. Although I didn't really know him, I wasn't sure if he was the sweet guy I wanted him to be, or the cold hearted killer that sent me the picture of the dead girl.

He could very well be the one who left the photo for me. It all fit together. He was there Monday when the photo was delivered, he could have returned Wednesday to see my reaction to his handy work, or this could all be mere coincidence and he really is who he says he is.

After about six hours, a detective called me by name. "Mackenzie Leigh, come with me please." The brown suit he was wearing looked like something he purchased in the seventies. "My name is Detective Rage." He spoke in an intimidating tone.

I turned and looked at Charlotte and Jillian as I stood in front of the cell door. I turned back as the clanging sound of keys entering the lock startled me.

A uniformed officer opened the cell door and let me out locking it behind me. I looked back at my friends one more time before turning down a hallway as I followed the detective to a small square room. In the center was a rectangular table with two chairs on one side and a lone chair on the other side. On the wall directly across from the single seat was a two-way mirror. That room was smaller than the cell.

"Have a seat Mrs. Leigh." The detective motioned toward the solitary chair.

I sat down and peered straight ahead trying to see through the mirror to the other side for who could be watching. All I could see was my own reflection peering back.

"You want to tell me what happened earlier with Officer Downing?"

"Is that what the lady's name is? What happened was a total misunderstanding."

"Please, help me understand." I noticed a hint of a southern accent.

"I wasn't trying to scare her. She was just making it difficult for me to report what I thought was a homicide." I told him my recount of the situation and gaining possession of the photograph. "And yet somehow here I am. Is there any way we can clear all this up so my friends and I, along with the gentleman we came in with, can go home?"

"Well Mrs. Leigh, if all of your stories match up and there aren't any inconsistencies, I don't see why not." He sort of half smiled.

"Have you heard about 'The Butcher'?" He asked.

"I have heard stories on the news about a man who kidnaps and tortures women that the press is calling 'The Butcher'," I mentioned vaguely.

"Do you know who this person is?"

"Why would I? How could you think that?"

"He obviously knows you. Why else would he send you a message?"

"I don't know. This person is evidently a psycho. Do I look like the kind of person who would associate with an unbalanced individual?" I asked.

"People aren't always who they seem to be. This person may be someone in your life you know, but don't know much about them. Is there any one you can think of who may have sent this to you? Perhaps, someone who has shown a strong interest in you even though you don't know them very well?" Detective Rage tossed the Polaroid down on the table in front of me.

I turned it over, not wanting to see the exposed state the woman in the photo was in. "There is only one person I can think of and you are already holding him here. I met Jasper Tully a week ago and I feel as though he may be stalking me, but there is something honest about him."

"I am going to speak with him. Just hang in there, I will be right back." He left the room.

I sat there wondering if Rage was accusing Jasper of being 'The Butcher'. Both options went through my mind.

If he were to confess, I imagined him sitting there with no emotion, no remorse, a complete lack of disregard for all human life. He would have no problem peering at any graphic photos of dead bodies in disarray.

If he really isn't the man they are talking about, I imagined him becoming sick to his stomach thinking that I accused him of being a killer, feeling shocked and betrayed. He would become angry and upset if Rage produced photos of mutilated women.

I regained control of my thoughts as the detective reentered the room. His posture was slouched and not as confident as before.

"Mr. Tully is not 'The Butcher'. There is no way he could be. We had to bring in a trash can. I showed him a few photos and he vomited. I am positive he is not the killer. Is there anyone else you can think of who could possibly want to cause harm to you?"

"I don't know." I placed my head in my hands, resting my elbows on the table.

"I still need to talk to the other two women with you." He placed a hand on my back, motioned toward the door of the interrogation room and escorted me back to the cell.

Next to be called in was Jillian. She stood, began walking to the door to the cell and fainted.

Charlotte and I rushed to each side of her. I lifted her head up as Charlotte fanned Jillian's face with her hand.

"We can allow her to compose herself. Mrs. Moore, please come with me," Rage said.

Charlotte was the strongest of the three of us. I wasn't worried about what she would say. Hopefully she prepped Jillian enough while I was being questioned. Now it was my turn to help my friend overcome her fear of being caught even though she was telling the truth. She would confess to anything if she thought they would leave her alone.

Once in high school she had walked into a bathroom just as three girls were walking out. What she didn't know was that those girls had been smoking in that bathroom. When she came out, the principal and a couple of teachers were in the hallway waiting on her. She was escorted into the office and questioned. She denied it at first, but after ten minutes she just wanted them to leave her alone and stop smelling her hair and clothes so she confessed. She spent three days in detention for smoking; we didn't want her spending any time in jail for murder.

When she regained consciousness, I helped her stand and walked her over the bench on the other side of the room. I sat down next to her as she gnawed on her thumbnail.

"Jilly, calm down," I said softly as I stroked her hair. "Just tell them the truth and nothing bad is going to happen. I promise. Trust me."

Gnawing on her thumb nail, jiggling her leg nervously, she just sat there with a look of fear on her face. She was lost in her own thoughts.

It wasn't long before Charlotte returned with the detective. "I'm telling you detective, none of us are mentally unstable enough to do something like this. Mackenzie just overreacts sometimes to certain situations and Jillian is always afraid she may or may not have done something. She seems to think everyone is out to get her. The poor thing gets so nervous; I bet she is chewing on her thumbnail right now."

As Charlotte and Rage stepped up to the cell door, they both peered in and began laughing.

"You hit the nail on the head," Rage commented.

"See, I told you," she said pointing at Jillian and me. I'm sure the expression on my face said it all.

"Alright, the three of you are free to go." The uniformed officer opened the cell door. He and the detective stepped aside to let us through.

"What about Jasper?" I asked.

We hadn't seen him since we were arrested. I was worried Rage had lied to me about talking to him. Maybe he really was 'The Butcher', but the detective made me feel sorry for Jasper. But what if he wasn't? What about him?

"Don't worry; he is being released as we speak. He will be waiting for you at check out." Detective Rage escorted us to the check out desk to collect our personal belongings.

Jasper was already there, waiting in one of the chairs that sat in a row of five, when we arrived. He stood. His facial expression changed from worried to relief. I ran up and hugged him. "Are you okay? Did any one hurt you?"

"I'm fine. Are you okay? I was so worried." He wrapped me tightly in his arms.

Finally some true affection, I thought. At least he didn't back away from me and try to shake my hand. Just then, I snapped back to reality remembering we still don't know who sent me that photo. I pulled away from him slowly so as not to raise any suspicion.

The moment the door to the police station closed, I turned to face Charlotte. "What happened? How did you get him to release us? What did you say?"

Jillian, Jasper and I stood around her in a triangular formation, facing her. We waited, staring, for her to explain.

"That's *my* little secret." She flashed a sinister smile then motioned for us to reenter Jillian's vehicle.

Five

It was well after midnight once we left the police station and none of us had had dinner the night before. We spent that time locked up. After a few minutes of discussion, we decided to go to the 24-hour pancake hut.

"Hello, folks. My name is Bonnie and I'll be taking care of you tonight. Can I get ya'll something to drink?" A waitress said as she pulled her server book out of her apron along with a pen.

"As a matter of fact we are ready to order too," Charlotte said as she rubbed her belly.

"No problem, I can take your entire order now." Bonnie crouched down next to the table and wrote down everything as we ordered.

"Seriously, Charlotte," I started after the waitress walked away. "What did you say to the detective?"

"What did *you* say to the detective?" She repeated.

"I asked you first," I childishly teased.

"I asked you second," she teased back.

"So you tell me first and I'll tell you second," I completed.

"I told him exactly what happened. The one thing I did tell him that you probably didn't think to tell him was that you felt you were being threatened and may have gone a little overboard with the female officer.

"It was just a misunderstanding. You were concerned for the girl in the photo and wanted to make sure law enforcement was aware of the murder and if it was at all possible if a patrol officer could keep an eye on your house. Those were the main reasons we even came in.

"He took in the explanation, nodded. He said he could understand the overreaction, we would be released and he would make sure a patrol officer would pass by your house every hour watching for suspicious activity." Charlotte raised her eyebrows and smiled like a goof at me.

"Super Charlotte to the rescue," Jillian laughed.

"Like always, if Charlotte can't fix it, well then it just isn't broke," I joked.

"What did you say about us? Why did you come back laughing?" Jillian asked Charlotte.

"Well, I told him that you," she pointed at me, "overreact about the simplest things. Jillian, I told him that you crack under pressure and might try to confess to a crime that he never asked about. Then I told him that if he and I walked up to the cell laughing, both of you would have the goofiest confused faces. That's when we came up laughing. Ya'll did look confused and goofy." She smiled at both of us.

The three of us had been laughing and joking for so long we never, even noticed Jasper had removed himself from the table. I looked around the restaurant and spotted him sitting at a booth four tables away.

"I'll be right back," I told the other two.

I stood up, walking over to where he sat, pondering what was upsetting him, I joined him at the table. "You've been quiet all night. What's wrong hun?"

"The three of you seem to know each other so well, I feel left out. It took you ten minutes before you noticed I had left," he pouted.

"Well honey." I touched his hand. "We have been together for the past fifteen years. We *should* know each other pretty well."

"I want to know you that well. I want to be the one you have inside jokes with, the kind that no one understands but us."

"We just met last week. The more time we spend together, the more we will learn and know about each other. Now come back and join us," I comforted.

He smiled at me, took my hand and we rejoined the others.

"We're back. What were ya'll talking about?" I asked as we resumed our seats.

"We were just discussing what we want to do when the sun comes up," Jillian informed us.

"I'm sure *I* will be sleeping, I don't know about you," I said giggling.

"You know what I mean. Instead of saying tomorrow, because technically it is tomorrow seeing as how it is one in the morning, I said when the sun comes up."

"To me…" I began.

"Yah, yah, it's not tomorrow until you wake up, we know," Charlotte interrupted.

"Do you see how annoying it can be to have someone know you so well they can finish your sentences?" I said facing Jasper.

He smiled. "I think it's sweet."

After we ate, Jillian took me home. "I think Jasper is a great guy. You should give him a chance."

"I think I may have to. He seems to like me and he also wants to get to know me."

"That's a good thing. He could be the one you know," Jillian said smiling as she pulled up onto the driveway of my house.

"That is the furthest thing from my mind, but I'll think about it," I said as I climbed out of the car.

Jillian watched me as I walked up the sidewalk to my front door. I turned the key inside the lock and heard the bolt slide back and into the unlock position. I opened the door then turned and waved before closing myself inside. I locked the deadbolt, waved to Jillian out the front window then headed to the living room to watch television.

The sun was rising and after all the excitement last night, I wasn't tired. I flipped on the morning news. The anchorwoman was reporting about the girl from the photo, finally.

"Another woman's body turned up today at the Memorial Hospital. She was in her mid to late twenties and found in a fifty-gallon plastic storage box. Her left leg had been removed just above the knee like the others.

"Some newspapers have named the killer 'The Butcher'. This is the fourth victim to date. The last two victims were murdered within two months of each other. Compare that to the first victim who was murdered five years ago.

"Each woman has been brutally beaten and tortured. The four murders are synonymous with a murder that took place twelve years prior to the first. The only difference was how it all ended. Corbin Townsin murdered his wife by removing her left leg and watching her bleed to death. He hung the leg in their dining room right over the dining table.

"Police say once Dina Townsin took her last breath, that's when Townsin used a gun to take his own life. Police have asked that anyone with information about these murders or 'The Butcher' please call the tip line at the bottom of your screen." The anchorwoman passed the attention over to the weatherman.

I turned off the television and sauntered upstairs to shower. I couldn't get the image of the woman from the photograph out of my head.

After I freshened up, I laid down in bed to get a little sleep. I kept thinking about the guy in the news report, 'The Butcher'.

When I drifted off to sleep, I began to dream I was 'The Butcher'. I felt as though I was seeing through his eyes, as if I was living inside him. I could feel his emotions.

He was watching the newscast that mentioned the murders and nickname. He became excited every time he heard someone discussing his work. He flicked off the television and smiled as he leaned back in a reclining chair. He sat and thought about how he would commence torture on his next victim and chuckled.

"Now that the police are looking for me, I am going to have to go on hiatus for a while, but because I have already sent that picture with the note, *your next,* on it I have to fulfill my promise," He said to himself, starring into the mirror. In my dream though, when he looked into the mirror, I saw my face.

I was looking at notes and pictures he had taken of me. He had a list of my activities and my schedule. In every picture, I had my long chocolate brown hair pulled up in a ponytail and my bangs swept to the left side of my forehead.

He decided he couldn't watch me any longer. He needed to have me. I could feel the urgency, his need to have me in his possession.

He turned around. His face was different. It was no longer my face. Just before the light shone on his profile, I woke up completely soaked in sweat.

I was so freaked out I decided to go for a walk around the neighborhood. I had slept most of the day. It was now early evening and the sky was a pinkish orange. It was beautiful. It was a comfortably warm evening with a slight breeze. The airstream brushed across my skin lightly before rushing off to the trees.

The foliage swayed back and forth as though it were waving at me as I walked by. I was so mesmerized by the horizon I didn't realize how far I was from home until I ran out of sidewalk. I turned around and headed back to the house.

As I perambulated toward my residence, I thought I heard footsteps behind me. I turned around, but saw no one. I shrugged my shoulders and continued. Two more times I was sure I could hear footsteps behind me. The only problem was every time I turned to look, no one was there. Maybe I was being paranoid. I walked faster to get home sooner. By the time I got there, the sun had completely set. I went inside, locked the dead bolt, slipped my shoes off at the bottom of the stairs then headed for the kitchen. Just as I reached the refrigerator, the doorbell rang.

I moved toward the front door and glared through the peephole, but again no one was there. I opened the door assuming I could spot the kids playing ding-dong ditch. I stepped down off the front porch leaving the door open so I could run inside incase it was someone else besides kids.

The concrete under my bare feet was still warm from the sunrays. I stepped carefully so as not to step on a rock or anything sharp.

I sauntered to the left peering between the houses to see if anyone was hiding there. I didn't spot anyone so I headed for the other side of the house. Before I had time to look, I heard the house phone ringing inside. I jogged back into the house, closed and locked the door, answered the phone.

"Hello?"

"Kenzie, it's Charlotte. Jillian and I have decided to go out tonight."

"I think someone is watching me. I don't really feel like going out. I think I'm freaking out. I could be abducted on my way out, or on my way home, or even while I'm at the bar. I'm not in the mood to go anyway, but thanks for inviting me," I told her.

"You should really get out of the house if you feel like someone is watching you. Maybe you shouldn't be alone. Come out with us and we will keep you safe. Afterward if you still feel the same way then you can stay at my house, how about it?" She asked, almost begging.

"Fine, but I'm on your watch and if something happens to me in that time then it is your fault. Guilt on you," I responded.

"No problem. I take full responsibility for your safety tonight. Get dressed up and meet us at our usual bar. We will see you in about an hour." She hung up before I could change my mind.

I headed upstairs to my bedroom, opened the closet door. Inside there was an outfit I had never seen before. The clothes had been separated right in the middle and on a double hanger was a lavender tank top and black pleated skirt.

"Where did this come from?" I asked myself aloud.

"Just put it on," a man's gruff voice insisted from behind me.

I started to turn around, but before I could get half way around, he was restraining me. His hands were holding tight around my waist.

"Don't turn around. Just put it on," he insisted again.

I took the outfit out of the closet and hung it on the doorknob. His grip was so tight I could barely move. I tried to escape to the bathroom to change, but he tightened his grip.

"Do it here, in front of me. I want to see your body."

I started to cry, but I didn't let him hear me. Tears were streaming down my face. He removed his hands and I began slowly to remove my clothes. I was standing in my bedroom in my bra and panties. I hugged my body, self-conscience about myself. He placed his hands on my shoulders then pulled me to him in order to smell my hair. He inhaled deeply.

I could feel his breath on my ear as he gave me more instructions. "Get dressed. Remove your undergarments first." He walked across the room and sat on the edge of the bed.

As I reach around to unhook my bra I thought I could hear him pleasuring himself. I figured if all he wanted was a quick thrill, I would just do what he wanted and hope he would go away. I allowed my bra to fall to the floor. Next, I pulled down my panties slowly so as not to startle him in anyway to cause him to hurt me.

I continued to cry as I pulled the tank top over my head and situated it on my body. I then stepped into the skirt, slowly pulled it up over my bottom and settled it onto my hips. I buttoned the three buttons on the left side then stood there waiting for further instructions. I hoped it was just another dream and I would soon wake up.

After a few moments, he was behind me again, wrapping one arm around my waist and covered my mouth and nose with a cloth. I tried to struggle but realized the cloth was soaked in something that smelled funny. Just before I blacked out from the fumes, I realized what it was.

Six

When I regained consciousness, I felt dizzy, light headed and my entire body felt heavy. I lifted my head up slowly and looked around. The room I was in had smooth concrete walls and floors. It appeared as though I were in some kind of basement. My mouth was taped shut and my arms and legs were strapped to a chair with silver duct tape. A chair in which could only be described as a dentist chair. It was just like in my dream. I was living in my nightmare.

I realized I was alone, but for how long? I attempted to pull my arms free. The tape was so tight I could feel my skin burning from the friction as I moved my arms in every direction possible, trying to loosen the bindings. Every muscle in my arms was being used which in turn caused them to cramp.

My heart was racing. It felt as though it would burst through my chest at any moment. I felt panic set in as I pulled harder and harder to try and get free.

A door behind me slammed shut and I froze out of fear. I couldn't move anymore. Within seconds there was someone standing directly behind me.

"Don't worry Mackenzie; you will know why you are here momentarily. For now I am going to tell you what I expect out of you," he whispered into my ear so softly I could feel the heat of his breath.

I couldn't see his face. It was so dark in the room and he seemed to be trying to stay behind me or in the shadows.

"If *you* promise not to scream, *I* promise to remove the tape over your mouth. Do…you…under…stand?" He asked, pausing between syllables.

I nodded noticing a slight southern twang in his voice. I guessed Tennessee or Georgia. He ripped the tape off in one quick pull. I groaned in pain. It felt like he plucked my lips off.

"Who are you? Why are you doing this to me?" I asked.

He didn't answer. He remained behind me, inhaling the scent of my hair. I turned my face away from his touch as he rubbed his fingers over my cheek.

He stepped in front of me and slapped me so hard across the face it blurred my vision. I groaned in pain, again. His face was covered by a ski mask. He squeezed my cheeks together with one of his muscular hands.

"Don't turn away from me." He moved his hands down and grazed them over my breasts, groping my nipples with his fingertips.

I squirmed in the chair still trying to get free as well as attempting to keep him from touching me. He cupped my breasts, one in each of his hands, then brought his face down and nuzzled between them. I felt violated.

To prepare myself from being slapped again, I gripping the armrests of the chair so tight my knuckles turned white. I closed my eyes so I couldn't see what he was doing, although I felt everything.

"Please, stop. Why are you doing this? Let me go," I yelled, still struggling.

He slid one hand down my torso stopping at the top of the skirt. He rubbed his hand back and forth across my stomach inching one finger down into the waistband and running it along my pubic line. I briefly held my breath hoping he would just have killed me right then.

He withdrew his hand only to move it under the skirt. He used one finger to lightly rub my private area as he continued to fondle my chest. I could hear him moaning in ecstasy.

"Do you like it when I touch you there?" He asked.

"Why are you doing this to me?" I asked again, tears streaming down my face.

"That's not the right question. The correct question would be how *long* am I going to do this to you?"

"Why?" I cried out loud. I thought about Charlotte and Jillian. Wondering what they must be going through, not knowing what happened to me. I had to stay alive if only long enough to see them one more time and tell them how much I cared for them.

I took deep breaths to calm down. I knew if I was all worked up and this guy stabbed me, the faster my heart beat the faster I would bleed out. I wanted to beat him at his own game. I wanted to do everything I could to stay alive.

He moved away from me and set up a video camera, aimed it at the chair I was strapped to and turned it on. He shot a few still photos with an old Polaroid camera.

"Now we are going to have some real fun." He walked over to me, pulled out a switchblade and cut the tape releasing my right arm.

He grabbed my arm and held it out in front of him straightening my elbow. He gripped one of his hands around my wrist, rubbed his other hand up and down my arm as if he were examining it. He stopped at my hand. Grasping my thumb tightly, he slowly bent it backwards until it snapped.

I screamed this time. "You broke my thumb, you bastard. Why did you do that?"

"Because I can," he said simply. He let go, cut the tape on my other arm and began the same ritual, only this time before he got to my hand I pulled it away.

He again slapped me, hard, across the face. I ran my hand over the spot and could feel my cheek welting. He grabbed a handful of hair in the back of my head and yanked me back so quickly I thought he might have given me whiplash.

I was staring right into his cold dark eyes. "I thought we went over this. Don't pull away from me." I could hear the anger in his voice.

The more mad he became, the more I noticed his accent disappearing. *Could he possibly be faking the accent so I couldn't identify him?* I thought.

He released my hair, but his nose was within inches of mine. I gathered as much saliva in my mouth as I could, leaned back away from him and aimed right into the eye holes of the ski mask. He flinched as the mucus came into contact with his ocular secretions.

He reared back his right arm as though he were going to punch me in the face. I scrunched up everything in my body and prepared myself for the blow. When it never came I opened my eyes and realized he was no longer near me.

He had walked over to shut off the video camera. I cradled the arm with the broken thumb close to my body. He came back over next to me with the silver duct tape in his hand then proceeded to re-tape my arms back to the rests of the chair.

I fought with everything in me not to allow him to bind me again. My arms flailed around like a crazy person in a nut house and all I could say was, "no", over and over. I was determined not to let him win.

He continued to grab for my arms as I moved them around like a sky puppet. My thumb flopped around as I redistributed the position of my arms in every direction.

Finally, frustrated and out of options, he climbed into my lap. Focusing all his attention to one arm at a time, he captured my right arm and pulled it down to the chair as I pounded him as hard as I could in the back with my other hand.

He shifted his focus to my only defense mechanism and was able to overpower me and strapped me back down to the chair. I was still struggling to get free when he stood in front of me and leaned into my face again. This time he placed a hand over my mouth.

"We can finish this later. I hope you will be eager to cooperate when I get back." He walked behind me and all I could hear were footsteps on wooden stairs.

Again, I tried to remove my arms from their bindings. The thumb on my right hand throbbed every time I wrenched it. I sat still for a moment trying to gather my thoughts and hatch a plan in order to escape this maniac in one piece.

I figured the best approach would be to free my left arm first then attempt to remove my right arm using the left one. I set my plan in motion by twisting and turning my left arm inside the tape. I assumed if I did it long enough the adhesive would wear out and I could just slide my arm right through. I didn't know if I had enough time to get all the way through the tape, but I was determined to try.

I could feel the stickiness balling up like glue as I continued for what seemed like hours – but may have only been minutes. My arm felt as though it were on fire as I squirmed faster and faster trying to free myself before he returned.

I could feel a warm liquid substance fill up between my arm and the tape; I hoped it was only sweat. Once it was loose enough, I slid my arm toward my body and released it. Unfortunately, what I thought was sweat, turned out to be blood. I had rubbed all the skin off the top of my arm from my wrist to my elbow. I ignored the burning sensation as I picked at the tape from my right arm carefully so as not to jostle my broken extremity.

I had to bite down on my lower lip to keep from yelling out in agony as I ripped the adhesive away from my appendage – one quick motion, like a Band-Aid. Once both limbs were free, I pressed my right arm up across my chest to keep from injuring my broken bone any more than it already was.

I leaned forward and began the same process to free my legs. The first one took me a few moments to get started as I tried to lie across my lap without crushing my wounded hand. Just as I finished with the first and started with the second, I heard the footsteps on the stairs again. He was coming back. I ripped and pulled as fast as I was able so I could fight him in order to escape.

I removed the last bit just as he reached the bottom. I stood up and turned to face him. He was still wearing the ski mask in order to conceal his identity.

"What the hell do you think you are doing?" He asked attempting an intimidating posture.

"I'm sorry," I said sarcastically. "I just prefer to have my thumbs intact."

He lunged toward me. I quickly maneuvered around the chair on the opposite side from him and sprinted into the shadows heading for the stairs. I could hear him running behind me. I reached the steps before he was able to catch up to me and headed for the light coming out from the bottom of the door at the top.

Once I reached it, I placed my hand on the doorknob. Just as I turned the circular brass I felt a strong hand on my shoulder. Without any notice, I was thrown back down the stairs. I landed hard on my back, smacking my head against the concrete floor.

I felt disoriented, a little confused as well. I couldn't move fast enough to get away at that point, so I just laid there.

He sauntered down the steps, knowing I could no longer fight him. He lifted me up, by my hair, into a standing position then slung me over his shoulder. My skirt flipped up exposing my buttocks.

"Naughty, naughty, naughty," he said as he smacked my uncovered rear end.

He stopped in front of the chair, but before putting me down he proceeded to touch me inappropriately again. I could feel him touching me. He rubbed his fingers around my private area and mumbled inappropriate words as though we were being consensually intimate.

Once the disorientation subsided, I tried to fight him to put me down. He smacked me one last time on my rear before dropping me down onto the chair in a sitting position.

"You are making this harder than it has to be, sweetheart," he said.

This time, as he tied me down, he jammed his knee into my leg, which caused me to only focus on how much that hurt compared to the fact that he was tying me with a rope first then duct taping over it.

Once he had finished with both my legs and my right arm, he held my left arm down to the arm rest and looked me in the eye. Before he could speak, I inhaled deeply, gathered more saliva, as much as I could conjure considering I was practically suffering from dry mouth. As I exhaled, I spit in his face, again.

Without speaking, he grabbed my wrist, went straight for my thumb and in one swift motion he broke it. Again, I screamed. He slapped me across the face again only this time with the back of his hand. Almost immediately, I felt my eye beginning to swell shut.

He walked around behind me and stroked his hands over my breasts again. After a few moments he stepped back up in front of me, gripping my face in his hand, squeezing tightly so I couldn't spit at him again, getting close enough to my face I could smell his breath, which was like onions and garlic mixed with the strong smell of cigarettes, he pressed his lips to mine.

"What are you going to do to me?" I asked as soon as he let me go.

"You will find out soon enough. Tonight you just need to get some sleep." He used more rope to tie my entire body to the chair so tight I couldn't move. "Now you can't escape. I'll see you in the morning." He headed to the staircase again, stepped up the stairs and turned off the light before leaving.

I couldn't see anything. I struggled as much as I could to get free until I ran out of energy. I was in excruciating pain. Both of my thumbs were broken, my left arm was raw and bloody from my first escape attempt and my head felt like there was a marching band with only drummers banging around in my brain.

Once I was too exhausted to move, I finally fell asleep in the most awkward position considering I was strapped to a chair.

Seven

I was abruptly awoken by the sting of a box cutter slicing my biceps and thighs. I braced myself and winced every time the blade came into contact with my skin. I could feel as the blood trailed down my arms and legs then dripped into a puddle on the floor. I remained disoriented, although not knowing if it was due to the blood loss or being jolted awake.

"Please stop. I can't take it anymore," I pleaded.

"Good morning, sunshine. How are you feeling today?" He asked.

"Violated and tortured. How am I supposed to be feeling?"

"Relieved," he said.

"Relieved, why?"

"The fact that you are with me, your one and only true love."

"I doubt that. I don't even know you." I had tears streaming down my face and when I spoke my words were winey like a child not getting their way.

"Oh, but you do know me. You know exactly who I am. If you thought about it long enough you might be able to figure it out." He set down the knife on a homemade wooden table. At *that* I was relieved, knowing that he would no longer be cutting me.

"Why are you doing this to me?" I asked, hoping to get a straight answer from him, but he only laughed. "I promise

I won't say anything to the police." He turned his back to me and I struggled to get out of the restraints.

I frantically twisted my arms to loosen the tape. Although he was still in the room, I made no effort to be secretive about my plan. My sudden burst of strength alarmed him. He turned back around. With his apparent size twelve steel toed boots, he stepped onto my toes and put all his weight into attempting to crush my bare feet.

I screamed as loud as my voice would allow until he retreated. Every part of my body ached in some way. I felt as though I had no fight left in me.

I attempted one last plea for my life. "I can make up a story to tell everyone if you just let me go. I could tell them I was involved in a car accident and when the airbags deployed it broke my thumbs. Then all the windows shattered and the glass cut me up. I will say anything if you please just let me go." My entire body went limp waiting for him to slap me again.

"That wouldn't be any fun. A made up story won't be as good as the real thing." I flinched when his hand came into contact with my face even though it was a gentle touch.

"Please, I have a family."

"You don't have any children. There is no one for you to take care of. *I* can take care of *you*." He laughed a sinister laugh.

My entire body began trembling. I knew he was going to try and kill me, but I didn't want him to have the satisfaction of knowing he was the one who had taken my life. I took a few deep breaths as he wiped the tears from my cheeks.

"The main event is set to begin tomorrow." He walked over and picking up the video camera, moved it to another room.

He cut the tape that bound my arms and legs and carried me into the other room. The video camera was aimed at a bed.

I was in so much pain I could barely see. He threw me on the bed, face up, and proceeded to tie me up the same as he had done to the girl in the photo. He fondled my breasts and private area for a while before just walking away. I was exhausted and figured since I was lying down on a bed I may as well get some sleep while he was away.

I wasn't asleep for long before I was awaken in a similar manner as before. He was cutting my face, arms and legs with slight precision. He was cutting over previous cuts cross ways and causing them to reopen.

"Please just leave me alone. Let me go," I pleaded with him.

"We are too far into this to quit now. I am going all the way and you can't stop me. The more blood you lose, the weaker you become and the easier it will be for me to finish what I set out to do." He turned to a folding table along the wall next to the door. He picked up a bottle of vinegar and poured it into a spray bottle. He proceeded to spray my limbs with the stinging liquid.

My entire body began to tingle and I couldn't control my movement any more. Every fiber of my body was beginning to feel numb. It was as though I could no longer feel pain.

"Please I can't take any more. Just stop, please." I felt extremely weak, almost as though I had no fight left. I wasn't willing to give him control.

"Oh honey, I am simply making sure you don't bleed out too soon." When he finished misting my skin, he picked up a towel and patted me dry as though he were taking care of me.

I could feel my body shutting down. I sobbed quietly as he saturated another cloth with a clear liquid. I struggled through my restraints, now crying hysterically. I shook my head back and forth as quickly as my strength could muster as I screamed, "NO," as loud as my vocals would allow.

He grabbed ahold of my face with one hand, squeezing so tight, I thought he would break my jaw. I gave in and held completely still, staring at his masked face with dead eyes as he stepped back up to the bed and hovered over me a moment.

"There are still a few hours before I am done with you, but until then I would like to have fun without listening to you pleading for mercy." He smoothed my hair back off my forehead before ensconcing my nose and mouth with the fabric.

I tried to fight, but the smell was too over powering and I passed out.

* * *

This time when I regained consciousness, he was standing next to the bed with a surgical table set up in front of him. Several weapons were lined up along the metal tray. Meticulously lined up were a butcher knife, a scalpel, box cutter, hedge clippers and a baseball bat lay across the top. There was a blowtorch setting in the middle, which seemed oddly out of place. I knew it was time.

He lifted each implement, meticulously placing each one in jar of transparent liquid as though he were sterilizing each one. Once he had that completed, he turned toward a lineup of large weapons, leaning alongside the wall, picked up the machete, and looked it over. Deciding he was not in favor of it, he placed it, blade down, back up against the wall. He then retrieved a hatchet, eyeballing it, nodded. This was apparently his weapon of choice. He stood holding it in front of a full-length mirror he had hanging on the wall.

"I usually stand here after the deed is done so I can see myself covered in blood. I always find it ironic." He smiled at his reflection.

"Ironic? How?" I asked, attempting to prolong the process as to give myself enough time to slow my heart rate so it wouldn't pump so fast. I attempted to free myself once again.

"Wouldn't you like to know, sweetheart," he laughed.

"That is why I asked. I really would like to know what happened to you to make you want to do something like this to a complete stranger. I mean, you don't even know me." I began to cry again as I struggled.

"But I do know you, sweet Mackenzie. I have been watching you for years and following you for weeks. We have been having a secret relationship. It was so secret in fact, even you didn't know about it. Sort of like a forbidden affair, if you will. It wasn't until I saw you with another man that I became jealous. It would have just been polite to have ended it with me first, before seeing someone else." His voice became angry.

"It's like you said though, our relationship was so secret even I didn't know about it. How could I have ended it with you if I didn't know about you?" One hand was almost free.

"That's beside the point. I was a lot nicer when I took you. With all the other girls, I haunted them as they walked alone in the darkness. Once I was sure they knew I was following them, I ran up and whacked them on the back of the head with a baseball bat rendering them unconscious.

"The sound the bat made on their skulls was like hitting a homerun. When their bodies fell, I would imagine the crowd cheering for me. I would picture myself running around each base then sliding home and winning the World Series. As I would hitch their limp bodies over my shoulder it was sort of my victory dance." He smiled at himself in the mirror again.

"Now wait a minute. What other women are you talking about? If we were supposed to be in a relationship, why is it okay for you to see other women?" I turned the situation on him as I struggled to free both hands.

"Don't worry honey. All these women were before you." He turned and picked up the baseball bat.

"How many others were there?" I asked, tears burning under my eyelids.

"Only about five have been found, but over my lifetime you are number thirty. Don't worry sweetheart, they are going to find your body." Lifting the bat, standing with a batters stance, taking a couple of test swings, elevating the bat over his head, he swung it fast and hard shattering my left kneecap.

I screamed out in pain. I pulled both my hands out of the bindings, interlaced my fingers and gave one good swing to his groin. He dropped to the ground like a sack of potatoes.

I tried to untie my ankles, unfortunately for me, without the use of my thumbs, it was impossible. My leg was bleeding from the blow and my hands were useless.

I was now breathing so heavily it sounded like I was in labor. There was one continuous thought running through my head, I am not going to let this guy decide when it is time for me to die.

All of a sudden he stood up. It happened so quickly I didn't have time to react. He placed his hand on my forehead, shoving me back down on the bed. Without warning the baseball bat came into contact with my knee once again.

He picked up the hatchet again and swung it as though he were chopping wood. I screamed until I could no longer feel the pain. It was almost as though my leg had gone numb. He chopped at my leg until it was only holding on by a few strands of muscle.

He picked up the hedge clippers and I closed my eyes. I could hear the four times he opened and closed the blades until my leg was completely severed. He took what he had cut off and left the room.

I focused on my breathing, slowly in and slowly out. I opened my eyes and leaned up as much as I could. Blood was pouring from my knee onto the bed and dripping on the floor. I couldn't exactly get away so I left my other leg tied up. I only wanted to stop the bleeding.

I knew a tourniquet would be my best choice, but I didn't know how long he was going to be gone and I didn't want him to hurt me anymore than I already was. I had lost so much blood I was beginning to feel woozy.

On the metal surgical tray placed next to the bed, I picked up the butcher knife and blowtorch. I used the torch to heat up the knife until the blade was almost orange in color. I took a couple of deep breaths to prepare myself for more pain. Tears were streaming down my face as I glared at the stump that use to be my left leg. I grabbed a leather strap and placed it in my mouth to bite down on it.

I quickly yet carefully placed the scalding blade against the wound. Once I had finished, I wiped the butcher knife off on the bed sheet. I placed the items back onto the tray in the exact meticulous way he had placed them. I was in a great deal of pain and light headed from losing so much blood, as soon as I was back in the same position I was when he left, I passed out.

When I regained consciousness this time he was carrying me. He had me cradled in his arms and placed me gently into a plastic storage box as though I were a sleeping infant.

I never let on to him that I was still alive. I just allowed him to do whatever it was he was going to do. He draped a blanket over me and I couldn't see anything through my cracked eyelids. He picked up the box and carried it, with me inside, out of his house. I could tell it was night once I heard the crickets.

"Hey man, what cha doin'?" A man's voice asked.

I heard him let out an irritated release of air from his mouth. "I uh…got some stuff I uh…gotta get rid of," my captor stammered.

"Tomorrow night the guys are coming over to hang out and drink beer. Can I count you in?"

"Yeah, sure whatever." He hitched the box up.

"Man that looks heavy. You need a hand?" The other man sounded closer to me now. I was afraid to make any kind of plea for help in fear that my kidnapper may try to kill his neighbor too.

"No, no. I got it," he said as I was placed down. "Back off man, I can do it." I heard the sound of a car door being shut, then there was only silence all around me.

A few moments later, another car door opened and shut. I heard the start of the engine. Apparently this is the time he is going to transport me to his drop off point.

After a few moments the vehicle stopped and the engine cut off. He got out and I waited for him to come around to get me. When he didn't come around the vehicle to retrieve me, I pulled back the blanket. Luckily, I wasn't in the trunk of a car, I had been placed in the back of an SUV. I looked around through the windows realizing he had stopped at a diner, which was small, with approximately five tables and ten bar chairs, a hole in the wall that appeared it had been in business for thirty years, give or take a few.

"Apparently mutilating women makes him hungry," I said aloud to myself.

I peeped out the window of the vehicle and spotted him sitting at the bar type area as though he were just another patron. My leg was throbbing with pain and my face was completely swollen on one side I could barely see out of my right eye.

He ordered then chatted with the waitress as she poured him a cup of coffee. I shifted in the box trying to take the pressure of my weight off my amputated leg. I could see numerous people walk past the vehicle. Afraid to put them in danger to endure the same hell I had been through, I just kept quiet.

I peeked back at him. Now he was eating a sandwich of some sort. He continued to chitchat with the server. Once he had finished he threw some money down on the counter, told the waitress goodbye then started heading my way again. I grabbed the blanket with my first and second fingers with each hand, pulled it back over my head and continued to pretend I was dead. I could tell my leg had begun to bleed again. The warm liquid was filling the tight spot.

The door opened and shut, the engine roared to life, he continued to drive to wherever he was planning to take me. He turned on the radio and began singing along.

"This used to be one of my favorite songs, Mackenzie. You will never hear another song again. You should have just accepted our relationship. You could have gone on living if you would have been a little nicer to me." He talked to me as though I were a ghost in the car with him.

Once he arrived at the spot, he got out of the car and came around to where I was. I closed my eyes as he pulled back the blanket and smoothed my hair back off my forehead where it was matted by blood. He gently stroked my head and leaned down to smell my hair.

"Sweet Mackenzie. You look so beautiful even though there is no life left in your body. I hope you enjoyed our time together. We will be together again soon. If I am caught, I am sure to get the death penalty," he said then kissed my blood-covered forehead.

He lifted the box with me inside and placed it on the ground. Before leaving, he honked his horn four times then pealed away. I began feeling light headed and could feel my blood pooling around me. Once more, I passed out from loss of blood and lack of nutrition.

Eight

My eyes fluttered open. I first noticed Charlotte and Jillian. Once I spotted Jasper standing over me, my heart began racing. I felt strong fear and tried desperately to get away from him. I was pulling myself up higher on the bed until the pain kicked in.

Charlotte grabbed Jasper by the arm. "Come on, let's go." She escorted him out of the room.

I continued to scream, "Please, just leave me alone! Somebody help me! He's here to get me!" I yelled at the back of Jasper.

"Get a nurse," Jillian said.

As soon as Charlotte opened the door, two nurses came rushing in, one was brandishing a syringe. As one nurse grabbed my shoulders and attempted to hold me down, the other inserted the needle into my thigh.

Within a few minutes my entire body relaxed and I no longer felt hostility.

"What did you give her?" Charlotte asked.

"It's a sedative called midazolam. It's fast acting, but doesn't last long. She is still going to be responsive," the nurse with the needle said before leaving the room.

"Do you know your name?" The nurse that had held down my shoulders asked as she shined a light into my eyes.

I looked around trying to figure out where I was. I noticed everything in the vicinity was synonymous with a medical facility.

"I'm Mackenzie Leigh. What's your name?" I said, my voice was hoarse from screaming.

"I'm Claire. Do you know where you are?"

"Well Claire, I would hope I am in the hospital after what I just went through." I held up both hands to reveal casts. The horrifying incident was burned into my brain; the whole ordeal continued replaying in my mind. "Did they fix my leg too?"

Claire pulled back the blanket covering my legs. To my disappointment, my left leg was still missing. "I'm sorry Mrs. Leigh. There was too much damage done. Even if the doctors had your leg they wouldn't have been able to reattach it."

I took a deep breath to stifle my tears, motioning for Claire to replace the blanket over my legs. "I would like to be left alone for a while please." I turned away from everyone and looked out the window.

"We are going to be right outside the door okay Kenzie? Holler if you need anything." Jillian patted me on the back.

Tears gushed from my eyes and soaked the pillow. I didn't know what to say to them and there wasn't anything they could say to me to make me feel better.

Just before the door to the room closed completely, I heard Claire say, "I guess we will try again tomorrow to get her on the path to acceptance."

Oh great, a twelve step program, I thought. Once the door clicked shut, I rolled over onto my back and folded over the cover to see what was left of my leg. I wiggled the nub as much as I could although it still hurt. It was bandaged at the site of amputation. I threw the blanket back over to cover up my horrible deformity.

"Why? Why did this happen to me? What did I do to deserve this?" I cried out.

I never wanted to get out of the bed. I just felt like laying there for the rest of my life. If I knew I was just going to be a burden to everyone around me, I would have let the maniac kill me. Surviving was only a good idea if he had planned to dump me in the middle of the woods.

The hospital room door opened. Two men in suits entered and stepped up to each side of the bed.

"Ms. Leigh, I'm detective Gollin and this is detective Metz. We would like to ask you a few questions. Is that okay?"

"Are you serious? I have just been able to evaluate my wounds. I don't want to talk to anyone right now. Can you please come back tomorrow?"

"Let me leave you my card. When you are ready to talk, give me a call and I'll come by to take your statement," Gollin said.

"Thank you, sir. I will."

As the two detectives were leaving, a nurse came in with a tray of food. She placed it on the rolling table and pushed it over to the bed.

"No thank you, ma'am. I'm not that hungry," I told her pushing it away from me.

"I'll leave it here for you just in case you do get hungry." She patted her hand on the table and left.

Charlotte and Jillian reentered the room. They walked over and sat down in the two chairs up against the wall under a five foot window.

"Aren't you going to eat?" Charlotte asked.

"I'm not really that hungry," I told her.

"When was the last time you ate?" Jillian inquired.

"I ate breakfast after we got out of jail, then I had a little something just before Charlotte called."

"Kenzie!" Jillian sounded panicked. "It's Sunday. That would mean you haven't eaten in three days."

"You need to eat. That son of a bitch who did this to you didn't feed you!" Jillian yelled.

"Wait a minute. You mean to tell me it has been three days?" I asked. "It seemed like hours. Long excruciating hours."

"Technically it was two. You were found last night right outside. They immediately began surgery and continued all through the night. They saved your life." Jillian sat on the edge of the bed.

"What kind of surgery?"

"They had to clean up your leg. There was a lot of material stuck in the wound. They also said it had been burned. The doctors had to reopen the sight and clear it out in order to fix it." Jillian reached out to touch my amputated leg and I smacked her hand away.

"Don't touch it. I burned it. I wanted to stay alive long enough to let you and Charlotte know why I didn't show up that night. I didn't want ya'll to be mad at me." Tears formed in my eyes.

"We weren't mad at you. We were worried about you." Jillian wiped the tears from my cheeks.

"Please, Mackenzie, eat something," Charlotte said trying to sound cheerful as she pushed the rolling table over to me.

She unwrapped the plastic utensils and tucked a napkin into the collar of the hospital gown; a fake smile was plastered on her face.

"What happened during surgery? Did they find any other injuries besides the obvious ones?" I asked as I pushed myself up the best I could into a sitting position.

"Eat first then we will bring the doctor in to talk to you." Jillian and Charlotte stood next to the bed faking happy.

They were keeping something from me and I didn't like it. I wanted to know what was going on. I picked at the food, mostly eating the essentials (fruit, veggies and pudding).

"So what is going on with Jasper?" I asked.

"What are you talking about?" Jillian wanted to know.

"Why is he trying so hard to hold on to me? I can barely do things on my own right now and yet he still wants to be part of my life."

"He really likes you Kenzie, just take it the way that it is and be glad he still wants to be with you," Charlotte harshly said.

I pushed the tray away from me and insisted they tell me what they were hiding.

"Let's go get the doctor." Charlotte grabbed Jillian's arm. The two of them rushed for the door to leave.

"Freeze," I said and they stopped moving. "Turn around and tell me what is wrong with me."

"Well…," Jillian hesitated. Before she could continue, the door swung open and Jasper was standing there.

"Hey there beautiful. How about we go for a stroll?" He produced a wheel chair and steered it over next to the bed. "Your chariot awaits," he said. "I have to put this on first, the nurse said."

He produced a sort of sock like item pulling it over my stump to protect the bandaging. He lifted me up out of the bed and placed me gently into the chair.

I smiled and blushed remembering how charming he could be. I forgot all about my friends and allowed him to remove me from the safety of my room.

He took me to an atrium area with a garden and a Koi pond. It was so beautiful and serene I actually forgot, just for a moment, that I was now an amputee.

Turning me to face him, gazing into my eyes, he made me feel special. It was almost as if he was staring into my soul. As his exquisite green eyes pierced through me, my whole body began tingling.

Just before I thought I was going to float away, he spoke. "Mackenzie Leigh, I want to be the one person you lean on, your shoulder to cry on, your rock, your everything. Together we can get through this and move on to the future. I will help you live a normal life and forget all about what happened." He leaned in to kiss me.

I put one of my casted hands out and placed it on his chest, stopping him. "Wait a minute. Why would you want to be with someone who may never walk again, someone who can't take care of herself and will have to depend on others to do things for her?" I asked, stunned.

Grabbing my hand and removing it from his chest, he pulled me closer to him. "I love your personality, your attitude and the way your nose crinkles when you ask a question." He smiled at me and again leaned in for a kiss. He pressed his lips gently to mine. I couldn't help, but to slowly close my eyes and let him take my breath away.

I snapped back into reality and pushed him away. How could a man this perfect want to spend the rest of his life taking care of me? "I need you to take me back to my room, now please. Now please." I tried to maneuver the wheel chair myself but without the use of my thumbs, it wasn't working.

I put my hands in my lap and started to cry. I was overwhelmed by his persistence. Within the last couple of weeks we had already been through more than most people go through in the first couple of years of marriage. Considering the fact that he still wants to be with me even though I am technically incapacitated was amazing and scary at the same time.

Jasper tried to hug me but I elbowed him in the ribs and covered my face with my wrapped hands. He grabbed the handles on the back of the chair and pushed me to my room. Picking me up, placing me back on the bed, he gently covered me with the blanket. When I started to cry again, he climbed into the bed with me and cuddled me, rocking back and forth.

I was glad he didn't speak, I didn't want to talk. I let him hold me. Feeling calm, relaxed and safe, I fell asleep.

Nine

When I awoke, Jasper still had his arms wrapped around me and he was sleeping. I gently grazed my fingers over his cheek. He took in a deep breath and opened his eyes. We were lying face-to-face smiling at one another.

"Hello handsome," I said breaking the silence first.

"Hello beautiful," he returned.

"I'm sorry about what happened before. I just don't want to be a burden to you."

"You would not be a burden." He grasped my face in his hands. "I want to take care of you. I love you Mackenzie Leigh."

I was stunned. No guy had ever said that to me before.

"How can you say that? You don't even know me?" I heard myself saying the same words I said to my captor.

"I know enough about you to have strong feelings for you. I want to get to know you, to take care of you, to love you. Please let me into your life," he said, softly.

"I want to believe you, I really do, it's just hard to believe you feel such strong feelings for me so quickly, I'm sorry." I shifted myself in order to face away from him.

"Mackenzie, I know it is hard to understand and I don't expect you to feel the same way about me, but I *do* love you."

"How do you know? How can you be sure that you actually *do* feel love?"

"When Charlotte called me and asked if I had seen you, I was just as worried as they were. She thought you had stood them up to go out with me. When I told her I hadn't seen or heard from you since breakfast, she asked if I would help look for you.

"Immediately, I dropped what I was doing to help. That was when I realized how strong my feelings were for you. When you opened your eyes and looked at me, I knew it was love."

I actually believed him and felt the same way even though we had just met. I felt as though I had known him longer, almost like we had been together before. At that moment, I wanted to tell him everything about my life and I wanted to know everything about his.

I started to cry again, only this time it was because I was happy I had found someone to love me. "I love you Jasper Tully." As we kissed, Charlotte and Jillian reentered the room.

"The police want to talk to you Kenzie," Charlotte said with a concerned tone.

Without taking my eyes off Jasper, I replied, "Send them in."

Two detectives entered. One was Detective Rage who interrogated us after we were arrested. The other was a younger man, possibly in his late twenties - most likely fresh out of training.

Detective Rage was the first to speak, "Mrs. Leigh, I am very sorry about what happened to you. I assure you, your house is on 24-hour surveillance to keep you safe. There are uniformed officers keeping watch over the hospital room as well as your friend's homes."

"A lot of good that's going to do me now. I have already been mutilated. I don't need you anyway. Jasper is going to take care of me and keep me safe." I nuzzled in closer to him so my head rested on his chest.

"As a matter of fact, as soon as she is released from here, she is coming home with me." He stroked my hair.

"Mrs. Leigh, is there anything you can tell us about your abductor? Hair color, build, any noticeable scars or tattoos?" Detective Rage asked.

"I don't know. He wore a ski mask over his face and it was dark in the room he held me captive. Are you planning to interrogate me again Detective, or can I get some rest? I have been through a really traumatizing ordeal here." I decided I was going to play the victim for as long as I could.

"I know this is difficult for you Mrs. Leigh, but it is easier for us to capture the perpetrator when the description is still fresh in your mind," the young detective said.

"I'm sorry, who are you?" I asked with enough irritation in my voice for the rookie to cringe a little.

"My name is Detective Winston." He extended his hand out to me as though he wanted me to shake it.

"What do you want me to do with that?" I asked revealing the casts on both of my hands.

He nervously retracted his hand and stepped behind Rage.

"Ms. Leigh, please help us catch this guy. Anything you remember is helpful," Rage continued the questioning.

"I don't remember much. Just the major parts, broken thumbs, missing leg," I said pulling myself closer to Jasper.

Kissing me on the forehead, helping me get more comfortable, he got out of the bed in order to escort the detectives into the hallway.

"I think this can wait until later guys. Let her rest. How about you give me your card and if she remembers anything, I'll give you a call." He shook hands with each cop as they left the room.

Returning to my bedside, he sat down in the chair and held my hand.

"You know sooner or later they are going to want to ask you more questions," Charlotte said.

"They are going to want to know what happened to you in great detail," Jillian told me.

I let the information, along with the events that led up to me being admitted into the hospital, mill around in my head before speaking, "Maybe when that time comes I will be suffering from a slight case of amnesia." I flashed them a sly smile.

"Is there a reason why you don't want the police to find the maniac who did this to you?" Charlotte asked pulling back the covers to show my stump.

Immediately I yanked it back over so I wouldn't have to see it then revealed my reason. "I'm afraid."

"Afraid of what?" Jillian asked.

I looked out the window. "I'm afraid that if this man knows I am still alive he will come after me again. I don't think I could live through the torture a second time." Tears welled up under my eyelids.

"Oh honey, don't worry about that. You have me, Jillian and even Jasper to keep you safe. He was so worried about you. As soon as we found out you were in the hospital, he wanted to see you right away. The moment you came out of surgery he refused to leave your side."

"He really is a great guy and he is even willing to stand by you and take care of you even under the circumstances." Jillian flashed me a partial smile. I've known her long enough to know that meant she was hiding something.

"What's going on? You know something don't you. Tell me what it is right now," I insisted.

"Let me go get the doctor," Charlotte said and headed for the door.

"No, you are going to tell me now!" My shouting must have alerted Jasper. He had fallen asleep, resting his head on my shoulder.

"What is going on?" He said yawning.

"They know something about me, but they won't tell me what it is. Every time I ask they find all kinds of reasons to leave the room," I whined like a toddler not getting her way.

"If one of you doesn't tell her, I will." Jasper tapped his foot.

"Fine, I'll tell her." Jillian took a deep breath. "While you were in surgery, the doctors performed a rape kit on you. The man, who abducted you...raped you. The doctor said it was too early to tell, but you could be pregnant." She bit down on her thumbnail and turned her back to me as if she were embarrassed.

As the facts sunk into my mind, I didn't know what to say. I laid there contemplating exactly what I would do at this stage in my life with a baby, especially one that was the result of an abduction and rape.

I waved my hand in a motion to tell them to leave me alone.

"Let me know if you need anything," Jasper said as he leaned to kiss me on the forehead.

The three of them left the room mumbling to each other. I wasn't paying attention to what they were arguing about; I just wanted them to leave me to my thoughts.

I always thought I would have a baby with someone I was married to and loved. This was just too surreal. If I did turn out to be pregnant, I didn't know if I would want to keep it. I couldn't get an abortion, that's just wrong. Although, I didn't know if mentally I could go nine months carrying a child then give it up for adoption.

I decided to turn to the one thing I knew I could do alone, prayer.

"Dear God, please don't let me be pregnant. I don't know if I could handle this responsibility alone. No matter how much Jasper says he loves me I know he won't be able to stick by me through this. I don't want to lose him. Amen." I said it out loud to make sure I was heard.

If any of my prayers were ever going to be answered, this would have to be on the top of my list. I was determined, now more than ever, to get out of this bed and stop feeling sorry for myself. It wasn't going to be easy with my hands in casts, but I was going to do everything in my power to do things myself.

I had this horrible feeling in the pit of my stomach that there was no way Jasper would want to have anything to do with me if I had a baby on top of my condition. I couldn't walk and I didn't have use of my opposable thumbs, although, he did know about the pregnancy when he took me out to talk. He forced Jillian and Charlotte to tell me so it can't be that big of a deal to him.

"Charlotte, could you come in here please?" I called.

She poked her head in the room. "What is it?"

"I want to talk to the doctor. Could you please bring him to me?"

"I will be right back. Don't move," she said laughing.

I giggled a little at her joke. I was glad at that moment for the light mood.

She returned approximately five minutes later with a man in a white medical coat. He glanced at my medical chart, which was hanging on the back of the door. Stepping over next to the bed, he checked my heart rate and blood pressure on the machine before speaking.

"How are you feeling today Mrs. Leigh? My name is Doctor Morgan," he said.

"I feel like I have been beaten up and had my leg chopped off. How about you Doc?" I said sarcastically.

"Well, I see your sense of humor is still intact. That's a good sign. Do you have any questions for me?"

"First off, how long am I going to have to wear these," I asked raising both hands.

"The casts will be on for about eight weeks. There was a lot of damage. We also had to put pins in your thumbs to get them back in line. After the casts come off and the pins have been removed we will talk about therapy in order to regain usage of your thumbs." He smiled at me as though it were going to make me feel better.

"What about this?" I pulled back the blanked to reveal a leg and a half.

"That will take longer. There was a lot of damage. During surgery, a kind of balloon was implanted in your thigh. Do you feel this?" The doctor took my hand and rubbed my exposed fingers over a spot just above the wound. "Every week it will need to be filled little by little in order to stretch the skin. The extra will be needed in order to close up the gaping wound."

Doctor Morgan's pager signaled he was needed. "Do you have any other questions? Are you in any pain?" He asked looking down at the small rectangular screen.

"No, physical pain, only emotional, thank you doctor." I shook his hand with my fingertips.

He turned to face me as he opened the door. "I will send in a nurse to clean and re-bandage your wounds. You just relax and take it easy. You have been through a horrific experience and you deserve it."

I nodded. "Thank you."

"One thing I don't understand is if the hospital did a rape kit on me, can't they just give the sample to the police?" I asked Charlotte. "The police could run the DNA sample and find the guy that way instead of needing my statement. I would never be in danger and it is the job of the police to find him anyway. I don't want to step on any ones toes."

"They may have, but the police still would like you to answer questions about specific traits or markings. The DNA profile won't reveal that unless this guy has been arrested before and he is already in the database."

I continued to touch what was the rest of my left leg. It still felt like my leg in my hands, but the sensation of my fingers on my thigh was different. It had already been three days, but I was still suffering from phantom limb syndrome and I wasn't sure how long that would last.

I was startled by a knock on the door. Claire poked her head in brandishing a first aid kit. "Hi, I'm here to change your bandages," she said.

She started with my face. The bandage on my forehead was peeled off along with the one under my right eye.

"How do they look? Are they healing?" I asked as she sterilized the wounds.

"They are looking better. I think that by the end of the month they should be completely healed." Claire smiled at me.

"Do you think they are going to scar?" I reached up and touched my face.

"I don't know. We will just have to wait and see." She replaced the bandages with new ones.

"I don't know why I am so worried about my face. I *am* missing my leg," I ranted.

"Would you like me to wait until you are asleep before I change the bandage on your leg?" Claire asked.

"You can do it now. I'll be okay." I leaned up as much as I could so I could watch. I turned to Charlotte. "Do you have your camera on you?"

"I always do. Why?" She asked.

"Will you take some pictures of it for me so I can see how it looks?"

Charlotte shook her head as she fished the camara out of her purse. She snapped one picture then just stood staring. Claire unwrapped my stump. Charlotte acquired a couple more pictures while the nurse disinfected it with antiseptic solution. I only flinched once when she hit a tender spot. Once it was re-bandaged, another photo was taken.

"Are you planning on going back home once you leave here?" Claire asked as she gathered up the supplies.

"No, I was going to stay with Jasper for a while until I could do more on my own," I replied.

"I hope things work out well for you," she said and left.

Charlotte walked around and stood next to me. She handed me the digital camera so I could look at the photos on the small screen. The first was of the dirty bandage. The blood was old and brown in color. I began feeling sick to my stomach. I tried to hold it down long enough to see the damage that was done.

The next was of my exposed stump. I glared at the photo. It looked like a wild animal had bitten and tore off my leg. It was sloppily cut. Some of the skin was longer than others. It started out black in color. As it was cleaned, the more reddish it became.

Seeing my leg from that angle was strange to me. It seemed like I was looking at someone else. The nausea subsided as I felt more detached from the photos. I asked Charlotte to take a picture of my face. As she aimed the camera at me, I didn't show any emotion. She handed it back. My face was unrecognizable. I was looking at a picture of someone I didn't even know.

I turned away from the tiny LCD screen and handed it back. Tears formed in the corners of my eyes. The silence in the room was comforting. Charlotte took the hint and left the room.

A few moments later, Doctor Morgan reappeared. "How's everything going in here?" He said, upbeat.

I looked at him with tears escaping down my cheeks. "Not that great."

"Is there anything I can do to make you feel better?" He asked.

"You could turn back time so my thumbs are intact and I have my leg, but if that's not an option I'll take something to get rid of the pain and suffering." I curled up into the fetal position – with the one good leg I had – and cried.

The doctor pressed the call button for a nurse to come in. He jotted down notes on my medical chart while we waited. Charlotte opened the door to the room with Claire right behind her.

The nurse was wielding a needle. She walked over to my I.V. and injected the liquid into the intravenous tube. It relaxed me almost instantly. I laid there with my eyes closed listening to Charlotte converse with Doctor Morgan.

"How long is it going to take her to accept her condition?" She asked.

"That can only be answered by her. Psychologically she has to be ready. Before we can release her she has to speak with a psychiatrist anyway."

"Is there anything we can do to help her along?"

"Just love and support."

Morgan and Charlotte left the room and I was able to drift off to sleep.

Ten

Days turned into weeks and weeks into months. Finally, the casts were set to come off. As I sat in the wheelchair, Charlotte wheeled me through the hospital to Doctor Morgan's office. She helped me onto the table.

"Mrs. Leigh, are you ready to have use of your thumbs again?" He asked.

"More than ready. Am I going to be able to walk with crutches right away or is there some kind of rehabilitation I am going to have to go through first?" I asked as he turned on the saw.

Before answering, the casts were removed and he asked me to wiggle my fingers and make fists. "Do you feel any pain or discomfort?"

"They're a little stiff, but other than that I think my hands are fixed." I opened and closed my fists faster and faster until I felt the stiffness subside. "Alright doc, let's get me some crutches to get me walking again." I smiled.

"Not so fast, Mrs. Leigh. We need to make sure you have muscle control and see how much weight you can handle. If you can't hold your own weight you can't use crutches." Morgan shrugged his shoulders at me. "Let's head on to the rehab room."

Charlotte helped me into the wheelchair. I shooed her away when she tried to push me. I placed my hands on the side wheels, took a deep breath and pushed. Pain shot through my hands and up my arms. I yelled in pain.

"Mackenzie, are you okay?" Charlotte asked. She knelt down next to me. "Please let me help."

She pushed me as I cradled my arms against my chest. Still feeling useless, still not able do anything for myself, tears welled up in my eyes. As we strolled down the hallway toward the elevator, I thought about Jasper. I decided to break it off with him when he came to see me. I felt as though there was no reason I needed to burden him.

When we reached the elevator, the doors opened without having to push the button. Jillian and Jasper were standing there, talking. I lowered my head and rubbed my eyes hoping they didn't see me crying.

"Hey honey, let's see. Show us your new and improved hands," Jillian said with a smile.

I attempted to smile back but I thought she could sense the sadness as I held out my hands. "I don't know about improved. They still don't work. The only good thing about this moment is the fact that at least I can wipe my own ass again," I attempted a joke. "Hey doc, can I get a minute with Jasper before I go? I promise Charlotte will take me and I will do everything I am told."

"I will give you fifteen minutes then you have to go. I will give Charlotte the rundown on what needs to be done then meet you there. If you're not there in fifteen, I will not give the okay for you to go home tomorrow," He smiled again.

"Tomorrow, really?" I asked.

"The psychologist says you have made some real progress."

"Don't worry, I will be there and have a positive attitude." This time when I smiled, it was genuine.

Jasper took the reins and led me down the hall to an empty waiting area. He parked me in front of one of the chairs and sat facing me. At first, all I could do was stare at him.

"What did you want to talk about?" He asked looking worried.

"Look Jasper," I began. "I think you should move on with your life and forget about me."

He opened his mouth to protest, but I held up one of my newly revealed hands and he sustained himself. "Look, all I'm saying is that this is a lot for me to handle right now. With all the stress I am going through, you shouldn't be expected to take care of me. It's not fair to you. I mean we barely know each other.

"Sure you've been great over these last three months, but it hasn't been long enough for you to feel obligated to stay with me. Please just forget about me." Tears came back with a vengeance. They were streaming down my face and dripping from my chin. I felt like all I did was cry. I just knew I looked like a mess.

Just when I thought things couldn't get any more awkward, Jasper got down on one knee in front of me and pulled out the most beautiful diamond ring I had ever seen. "Please marry me Mackenzie. I want to be obligated to take care of you. I want to spend the rest of my life with you."

I sat there stunned. I didn't know what to say. We had only been on two real dates. I was shocked and speechless. I thought about trying to get away but I remembered how badly it hurt the last time I tried to wheel myself.

"I don't know Jasper. This is all so sudden. Like I said, we barely know each other." I touched his face.

"I want to know you. I want to know everything about you. Please allow me to spend the rest of my life getting to know who you are." He gently took my hand from his face and cupped it between his palms. "I love you Mackenzie Leigh."

"Jasper, please. Shouldn't we know more about each other before we get married?"

"I figure we can get to know all the good stuff about each other during the engagement. Once you are finished with physical therapy and you can walk on your own, then we will get married and we will know enough about each other to feel comfortable enough to get married." He kissed my hands.

At that point, I realized I really loved him too, but I didn't want to be his problem. I had run out of excuses and had nothing else to say except, "Yes, Jasper Tully. I will marry you." I smiled at him as he delicately pushed the ring onto my finger.

He stood up, but leaned down to embrace me. He wheeled me back to where Charlotte and Jillian waited.

"Guess what," I said as we approached.

"What's up?" Jillian asked.

I held out my left hand exposing the diamond positioned on my third finger. "Jasper asked me to marry him."

The three of us screamed in unison. I had a smile on my face so big my cheeks hurt.

"That is wonderful news," Charlotte said. "Let me see."

The four of us entered the elevator and rode it to the second floor as Charlotte held my hand staring at the ring. When we entered the therapy room, I noticed everyone there was suffering in some way. One man had just had knee surgery and was learning how to put pressure on it again.

Across the room, a little girl was missing her right arm just below her elbow, a weight was strapped to her nub and she lifted it as high as she could. I watched her for a while. She had such will and determination. She looked to be about eight years old. The little girl spotted me and began striding toward me.

"Hi, my name is Hailey. What's yours?" She said.

"I'm Mackenzie. How old are you?" I asked.

"I'm nine, but my mom says I'm going on nineteen." She giggled.

I smiled then asked, "Is it hard getting used to?" I pointed at her missing limb.

"It was at first, but Mr. Paul is helping me. He has made it easier." She gestured at a man who was heading our way.

"Hello Mrs. Leigh. I'm Paul McConnell, the physical therapist," he said as he approached to join the conversation.

I knew I had just become engaged, but Paul was incredibly handsome. His brown hair was beautifully manicured and his sparkling blue eyes were mesmerizing.

"Please call me Mackenzie," I said, blushing.

"Well Mackenzie, Doctor Morgan has informed me you are leaving tomorrow. I hope you are ready to get back to your life. First, I am going to start you off with the squeeze balls. Squeeze these, one in each hand, two to three hours a day at fifteen to twenty minute intervals. Do you have any questions?" He handed me two soft red balls that fit just right in the palm of each hand.

"How long am I going to have to do this? Is it going to take days, weeks, months?"

"It depends on your progress. When you can finally push yourself in here to see me, then we can discuss the next step." He smiled and it lit up his face.

"What would be the next step?"

"We would start you walking with crutches. Once you are used to those and feel comfortable doing that we will look into fitting you for a prosthetic leg."

"What will the prosthetic do?" I asked as I squeezed.

"It will be your new leg, just like when I get my new arm," Hailey said as she wiggled what was left of her arm.

"That makes sense. Maybe we can help each other get use to our prosthetics when we get them." I smiled.

"I'd like that, thanks Mackenzie." She skipped away.

"Thank you Mr. Paul. I look forward to working with you." We said our good-byes.

As Jasper pushed me back to my room, I squeezed on the balls until my hands hurt. When we arrived, he lifted me out of the chair and placed me onto the bed. Claire entered the room wielding my lunch.

I tried my best to use a fork while Charlotte and Jillian ping-ponged ideas back and forth about how my wedding should look.

"What about bluebonnets and baby's breath?" Jillian asked.

"I don't think you can get bluebonnets. I think they are only wildflowers. I don't know if any flower shop would have those," Charlotte said.

"I think daffodils are more of a wedding flower any way," Jillian told her.

"I think lilies are. The center pieces would look better with them."

"The center pieces are the least of our worries. We should be thinking more about the bouquets and boutonnieres. The wedding party's flowers should be daffodils."

"If that is what you are thinking then the wedding party should carry lilies."

"Lilies are not wedding flowers," Jillian argued.

"You think daffodils are? Maybe you should look at more wedding magazines. I had lilies at my wedding," Charlotte countered.

"I had daffodils at mine, so I guess we are just going to have to agree to disagree."

"Okay girls, that's enough. How about Jasper and I decide what kind of flowers to have? Ya'll go home and get some rest. I'll see you in the morning," I told them.

"Alright, have a wonderful night, we will be back first thing," Charlotte told me as she bent down over the bed to give me a hug.

Jillian hugged me and kissed me on the cheek. "I'll ride with Charlotte. We should both be here at the same time. Don't over sleep or we will jump on the bed."

We all giggled. They left the room and Jasper climbed into the bed with me and wrapped his arms around me.

"Once you are released, how about we go to your house, pick up a few things you might need and take it back to my house. We can get the rest of your stuff later," Jasper said.

"I won't be able to go into that house alone. I will need you to help me. I don't even know if I am ready to go into that house at all." I pulled him close to me and smothered my face into his chest.

"Don't worry; I will be with you every step of the way. I will never leave your side." Jasper ran his fingers through my hair.

"As long as you will be there with me. I will talk to Jillian and have her go over and set up the house to be sold."

"If the house is sold before the wedding, we can just consolidate our stuff. After we are married we can figure out what stuff each of us is willing to part with and sell it." He kissed me on the top of my head.

Just then, Doctor Morgan entered the room.

"Mrs. Leigh, I am going to need a urine sample from you to determine whether or not you are pregnant as a result of the rape." He looked down at the small cup he held in his hand.

I was dreading this day. I already knew the answer. Claire had told me that as a result of the tragedy, I could miss a couple of months of menstruation. I just knew the test was going to come back positive.

I accepted the specimen cup from Morgan. Jasper carried me to the private bathroom, placed me on the commode and stepped out, closing the door behind him. As I relieved myself into the small container, I could hear them talking.

"So tell me Doctor Morgan, what are the chances of her being pregnant?"

"Mr. Tully, I assure you her chances are just as likely as someone who was involved in consensual intercourse. Are you sure this is something you are willing to deal with?"

"If she can handle it, well then so can I. I am willing to stick by her no matter what."

Tears of happiness formed at the corners of eyes. A knock on the door startled me.

"Are you finished sweetheart?" Jasper's voice broke through the door.

"Yes, you can get me now," I answered back.

He opened the door, helped me cover my private areas then carried me back to the bed. I handed the cup back to Morgan.

"Once the test is completed, I will send Claire in with the results. It is similar to a home pregnancy test. It should only take between three to five minutes," the doctor explained.

When the door closed, I grabbed Jasper's hand. "I heard you talking to the doctor. Thank you for what you said. I love you Jasper." I kissed the back of his hand.

"I love you Mackenzie. I am going to stick by you no matter what the results of the test are."

It was the longest three to five minutes of my life. Once Claire entered, the look on her face told me what I already knew.

"Mackenzie, the test came back positive. You *are* pregnant." She came over and placed her hand on my shoulder attempting to console me. "I'm so sorry."

"I'm fine with that. Thank you." I motioned for her to leave. "Jasper, would you please hand me those squeezie balls. I am going to get out of this bed and walk again. I need to be able to take care of our child."

I didn't know what to say to him. I wanted to tell him to run as far away from me as he possibly could and not look back, but I knew he wouldn't leave me. I was terrified. How would I feel about the baby once it was born? Would I resent him or her? Would I pull away so I wouldn't love him or her? I wasn't sure how I would react once the baby was born, but I knew at that moment I wanted to abort the thing.

I squeezed until my hands cramped again. I handed the balls back to Jasper then settled in to take a nap.

Eleven

Feeling ecstatic, the freedom of home, knowing I would never be the same, I was delighted to leave the hospital. I may have had only one good leg, but I was being allowed to take home the crutches and wean myself into walking. After all the paper work was signed, Jasper took me out to his car. Doctor Morgan, Nurse Claire and Doctor Kimball, the therapist I was forced to talk to, all had to say good-bye before they would let me leave.

"Your progress is going well, just continue strengthening your hands so you can walk with the crutches on your own," Morgan said as he hugged me.

"Good luck sweetie," Claire said.

"When you come back for your last session I will refer you to someone you can talk to permanently. This will take a long time to get over. I urge you to continue with the therapy sessions even though they are no longer mandatory," Kimball informed me.

I agreed and Jasper helped me into the passenger seat before going around and placing the things I had accumulated while in the hospital along with the wheelchair in the trunk. I was pulling the seatbelt over my shoulder when I saw Paul running out of the hospital toward me.

"Mackenzie," he yelled as he approached the car. "I'm making an appointment for you at the beginning of next week to come see me. Within a month if I see significant progress, you will be fitted for your prosthetic leg. I look forward to seeing you next week." He smiled, hugged me and went back inside the hospital.

"What did he want?" Jasper asked irritated through the open driver side door once he came around to the front of the car.

As I told him about the appointment, he slipped in behind the wheel. I leaned over and kissed his cheek. He grabbed my hand and held it in silence to my house.

When he pulled up in the driveway, I was hyperventilating. "Jasper, I can't do this. I can't go inside. Let's just go, I want to leave."

"Calm down Mackenzie. If you don't want to go inside you can stay here and I will go inside and get you some clothes and stuff." He stroked my hair as I cried uncontrollably. All I could think of when I saw that house was how I was violated in my own bedroom.

"No, you can't leave me here alone. He could be anywhere, waiting. I can't go through that again. Please let's just go to your house. I'll get my stuff later." I pulled my one good leg into the seat with me and hugged my knee.

"Don't worry honey; we don't have to go in." Jasper put the car in reverse and headed to his house. "We can call Charlotte and Jillian and have them bring you some clothes."

Once we arrived, Jasper pulled out the wheelchair and came around to my side. He helped me out of the car and ushered me in to the living room. "You want to watch some television?"

"Only if you promise to hold me while we watch." I smiled at him in a way to hint that I didn't just want to watch T.V.

He flipped through the channels. "You wouldn't mind if we watched the news, would you? I want to see if the police have any leads from the DNA sample that was taken from you," he said.

"I don't mind at all. I'm a little curious as well." I cuddled up into his arms.

The news cast had just begun as we settled into the sofa. "New at five, the latest victim of 'The Butcher', Mackenzie Leigh, has survived the brutal beating and torture endured while being held captive for two grueling days. Leigh, who was released from the hospital earlier this afternoon, was discovered outside the morgue. Her body had been stuffed into a large plastic container.

"Leigh sustained severe damage to her left leg where 'The Butcher' amputated it just above the knee. There were also several cuts all over her body and major bruising to her face. Doctors were able to determine she hadn't suffered any bleeding in her brain or internally.

"Leigh is still in need of several physical therapy sessions before she can be fitted for her prosthetic leg. Doctors are optimistic she will again be able to live a normal lifestyle. Police have no leads as to whom 'The Butcher' is or his where-a-bouts." The news anchor passed the report on to the weather man.

"NO!" I yelled.

Jasper flicked off the television. I sat up and pushed away from him.

"This is not happening. Who would have told the press? Not only that I survived, but the other information as well?"

"I don't know Mackenzie. Calm down sweetheart," Jasper said as he tried to pull me to him.

I wrapped my arms around him. "What am I going to do if he finds me?"

"How is he going to find you? He doesn't know where you are. He can only assume you are staying at your own house."

"He knew about you. He said he had been watching me and if I had just stayed single none of this would have happened."

"I am not going to let anything happen to you. As long as I'm around you will be kept safe." He kissed me on top of my head.

I shrugged my shoulders and hoped he was right. I reached for the phone and called Charlotte.

"Hey Char, I need you to get Jilly and go over to my house and grab me some clothes."

"I thought you were going to do that on your way to Jasper's house?" She said.

"I couldn't do it. I couldn't go inside and I didn't want to be left alone in the car. That place freaks me out now. Just please do this for me," I practically whined.

"Okay, no problem. We will be there soon," Charlotte agreed and hung up.

"Charlotte and Jillian are on their way. They should be here soon," I told Jasper.

"Did you want to do something for dinner?" He asked.

"I don't know. Let's wait for them to get here so we can discuss it with them. Maybe we can eat out on the back patio seeing as how it is such a wonderful evening."

"We could. I think that would be nice. How about you help me set up the back yard so we can be ready when they get here?"

He stood up, lifted me off the sofa and place me gently onto the seat of the wheelchair. Wheeling me to the kitchen, grabbing a tablecloth and clips, Jasper prepared for our outside feast. He took me out to the patio and I handed him everything one piece at a time as he needed it.

"The tablecloth hooks are a nice touch," I said as he shoved the last one into place.

"With there being a slight breeze and all I figured we would need them." He kissed the top of my head just as the doorbell rang. "Let's go see if that is the girls."

He wheeled me through the house to the front door. Charlotte and Jillian had not only brought almost the entire contents of my closet, but also dinner.

"We were just discussing what we were going to do for dinner. Good call ladies," Jasper said handing me off to Jillian as he took the food from her.

Jillian and I proceeded to the patio as Jasper grabbed plates for the four of us and Charlotte dropped my bags off in the spare bedroom. I helped set the table as much as I could while the others divvied out the food.

"What happened today? I thought you were going to pick up clothes on your way here?" Jillian asked as we ate.

"Like I told Charlotte, I just couldn't do it. All the details from that night came rushing back like it was just yesterday. I don't know if I will ever be able to go back there," I explained.

"Why don't you just move out of the place? My name is on the mortgage too. I could talk to the real estate agent Mr. Moore and deal with the entire house issue for you," Jillian suggested.

"What if something was to happen before Jasper and I get married? Where would I go?"

"What is going to happen? What are you worried about?" Jasper asked.

"I don't know, anything," I said as I picked at my food.

"Don't worry Kenzie. You could always stay with one of us until you find another place," Charlotte said shooting Jasper her mean face. Her eyebrows furrowed, nose crinkled and lips puckered.

"Charlotte, relax your face. I'm only saying because the news announced today that I was released from the hospital. If this psycho is crafty enough to figure out where I am staying and where Jasper lives and does something he can't handle and decides I have too much baggage then I could be without a place to stay. That's all I'm saying."

Jasper turned toward me, cupped my face in his hands, looked me straight in the eye and said, "Mackenzie, there is nothing in this world anyone can say or do to change my mind about marrying you. I love you, end of story." He kissed me, pressing his lips gently to mine then went back to eating.

"Don't worry Kenzie, we will *all* make sure you are always safe and that 'The Butcher' never hurts you again," Charlotte told me reaching across the table to touch my hand.

"Thanks you guys. I don't know what I would do without you, any of you." I referred to all three of them.

* * *

During one of my therapy sessions a few weeks later, Paul decided I was making some real progress. "Your doing great Mackenzie. Keep on coming."

"When do I get my new leg?" I asked as I reached the end of the even bars.

"Twenty minutes. Are you ready?"

"Most definitely, you know it. Are you coming with me?"

"Of course I am. I wouldn't miss it for the world." Paul put his arm around my waist and helped me over to a chair. He leaned down and pressed his face to the top of my head and inhaled deeply as though he were smelling my hair.

"What are you doing?" I asked.

He kissed the top of my head and stood up quickly, possibly a little too quickly. "I was just giving you a kiss of encouragement." He said nervously as he pushed me over to where Jasper was waiting with the crutches.

Jasper stood up and tried to help me stand. Paul placed his hand on my shoulder to keep me in the chair and shook his head.

"She needs to be able to get up by herself." Paul smirked at Jasper.

"I don't think she is ready to do that yet." Jasper attempted to help me up again, but Paul stopped him once more.

"I have seen her progress. I think she can." Paul stepped up to Jasper.

"She lives with me. I see her more than you do and I say she can't." Jasper stepped up to Paul.

"Would you two stop talking about me like I'm not here? Now Jasper, hand me those crutches so I can get up, by myself." I placed a hand on each of their stomachs, pushing them apart.

I used all of the strength I had in both arms and my one good leg to pull myself into a standing position. I placed the crutches under my arms and headed for the exit. Paul led the way to the prosthetic wing of the hospital. Jasper followed behind me. Once we arrived, little Hailey was leaving with her new arm.

"Hi Mrs. Leigh. Do you see my new arm?" She asked holding it up for me to see.

"That looks great. How are you doing with using it?" I touched the plastic fingers.

"I still need a little work on muscle control, but other then that it feels like I'm whole again." A smile spread across her face.

"I'm going in for my leg now. Wish me luck." I smiled back.

"Maybe when you feel comfortable walking on your own again, you could walk to my room and show me."

"I definitely will."

Hailey skipped off and the three of us went in for my new leg. We were told to go right back to the fitting room and have a seat. I sat up on the table just as I had a month ago to have my stump plastered and measured for a perfect fit. The doctor came in with my leg in his hand.

"Are you ready?" He asked twisting it back and forth in his hands as though he were about to begin dancing with it.

"As ready as I'll ever be." I stuck out my stump and Doctor Morgan slipped on a sock like piece over my thigh before pushing the leg on over it and strapping it down.

"How does it fit?" He asked as my hamstring and quadriceps muscles worked together to move the prosthetic up and down. "Now stand up and tell me how it feels."

"You are going to have to have extreme muscle control in order to move the leg. Lift it up and see if you can swing it back and forth at the knee," Paul told me.

Hesitantly I stood, put slight pressure down on it but mostly leaned on Jasper. "I'm scared to do this on my own. I want my crutches," I whined.

"No Mackenzie, you have to do this without them. This is what you have been looking forward to since that first day in physical therapy." Paul took both my hands from Jasper's shoulders and like a toddler learning to walk, he let go and backed away. "If you think it will help we can try this on the even bars."

"I think it *would* be easier. Can I please have my crutches until we get there?" I could feel the tears welling up. I tried to blink them away but all that did was cause them to roll down my cheeks.

"It's okay Mackenzie," Jasper said as he hugged me.

"You can use your crutches to get back to the therapy room, but once we get there you have only the even bars to help you," Paul insisted sternly. "You were doing so great this morning. I know you can do this. By the end of the week, when you come back for your next session, I want you to walk through those doors on your own." Paul thrusted my support sticks at me.

"I will try," I said as I settled the crutches under my arms.

"I will help," Jasper told me pressing his lips to my forehead.

With a little hesitation, I moved one foot at a time. Slowly but surely I made it out of the doctors office. With ease and grace it took me longer then usual. After about twenty minutes of walking back and forth on the even bars, I was able to walk with the aid of only one crutch.

"Congratulations Mackenzie, I knew you could do it," Paul encouraged.

"You have made great strides here today. I think it is time to go home," Jasper said as he helped me out to the car.

"I will see you on Thursday, you hear me?" Paul said on our way out.

"I'll be here and I hope to be walking on my own."

Twelve

A couple of days later, I woke up in the middle of the night screaming.

"What's wrong? What happened?" Jasper asked as he grabbed hold of me and pulled me into his chest.

"Nothing, I'm fine. It was just a nightmare. No big deal," I told him as I grasped onto him as tightly as I could.

"No big deal? You woke me out of a dead sleep. It is a big deal. Would you like to talk about it?"

"No, I'll be fine. I don't want to talk about it. As a matter of fact I would like to just forget about it." I sat up, pulling away from him.

"You should really talk to someone about your nightmares," Jasper said as he rubbed my back.

"I'm fine. Eventually they will go away and I can forget all about them," I told him.

"The fact that your subconscious mind continuously replays your kidnapping and torture night after night really worries me."

"I promise it doesn't bother me that much. Sooner or later this will be a thing of the past." I kissed his cheek.

"Honey, you have been through a traumatic and horrific ordeal. You should really talk to someone about it. What about the guy Doctor Kendall referred you to? Maybe he could help get rid of the nightmares sooner rather than later." He wrapped his arms around my shoulders.

"I don't know who I can trust after someone leaked to the media I survived and they announced it on the news. How am I supposed to talk to someone if I think they will tell everything I say to the press?"

"We will talk to a few psychologists, do background checks and investigate their ethics before we choose one," Jasper reassured me. "They are supposed to keep everything to themselves about their sessions."

I nodded then stretched out next to him. I sprawled awake in bed for about ten minutes before having to get up and move around. I just couldn't fall back asleep. I got up and went to the kitchen using the crutches rather than taking the time to strap on the prosthetic.

I made some coffee then perused over the parenting magazine Charlotte and Jillian brought over. My eyes may have been scanning the pages but my mind was replaying the horrific ordeal I had lived through. Even eight months after the tragedy that resulted in the loss of my left leg, the details were still so vivid in my memory.

I decided it was time to set it free. Jasper had purchased a notebook the first night he brought me home from the hospital. He told me if there was anything I could remember about the incident, I should write it down. I never told him, or anyone for that matter, that I remembered everything.

I made every one think I could only remember bits and pieces so they would stop asking questions. I did not want to relive it every time the police needed me to answer some questions. It was just easier to tell them I don't remember so they would leave me alone.

I took the notebook out of the top drawer of the desk, which was located just behind the dining room table. I placed it, along with a pen, in front of me on the table. I said a prayer before opening the cover and scrawling out, detail by terrifying detail, the events that transpired.

Six cups of coffee, thirty-five pages and four hours later, Jasper entered the kitchen. By the look on his face, I could tell he was still a bit groggy.

"What are you doing sweetheart?" He asked, yawning.

"I remember everything. I wrote it all down and think we should take this to the police." I handed him the notebook.

He poured himself a cup of coffee then joined me at the table. He sat quietly reading while I crutched my way back to the bathroom to shower. I sat down in the tub and allowed the water to run over me. I felt like a helpless child not being able to stand and take a grown up shower.

I toweled off then crutched into the bedroom and sat down on the bed. I wondered how long it was going to take me to get used to having to attach a leg to my body. I still wasn't comfortable walking on my own yet so I took one crutch with me just in case.

Once I was dressed, I rejoined Jasper at the table. I watched his facial expression change from fear to completely horrified as he reached the end.

"We need to take this to Detective Rage immediately. Give me five minutes to shower and dress. Don't worry Mackenzie, even if I have to involve myself in the investigation, I will make sure the asshole that did this to you is caught." He practically sprinted down the hall to the bedroom. Precisely seven minutes later he was ready to walk out the door.

When he opened the door, I almost tripped over a box on the opposite side of the threshold. Glued to the top of the box was my name that had been cut out letter by letter from a magazine. Jasper lifted the box and I followed him to the sofa.

At first, we just sat staring at the box as though it were a foreign object. I didn't know what to do with it. I wondered where it came from, whom it came from.

"Are you going to open it?" Jasper asked as though he could hear my thoughts. He never took his eyes off the package.

"I don't know. Do you think I should?"

"We should at least know what is inside before we just show up at the police station with some strange box. They could laugh at us if it is just a package from your coworkers. You *do* work at a newspaper. Maybe they are sending you a present to wish you well."

"It wasn't sent here, Jasper. It doesn't have an address on it, just my name. Also, I was a surviving victim of a notorious serial killer. What if it explodes when I open it? Maybe it is something the bomb squad should look at first."

"Maybe your right. Grab the notebook. I'll get the box. Let's go."

He drove carefully, with the unopened parcel on the back seat, directly to the police station. I called Charlotte and Jillian on a three way call.

"We need ya'll to meet us down at the police station," I told them.

"What happened? Did they find him? Do they have someone in custody?" Charlotte asked.

"We received a package at the house and there is just something creepy about it."

"We'll be right there," Jillian confirmed.

I hung up the phone as Jasper pulled into the parking lot of the police station.

"We need to see Detective Rage," Jasper blurted as we approached the front desk.

"Have a seat. I will let him know you are here." The officer pointed to a row of chairs that were nailed down to the floor.

We sat down and waited. Jasper placed the package on the floor at his feet. It wasn't long before Charlotte and Jillian joined us. Before either of them could say anything, Detective Rage approached.

"Mrs. Leigh, what can I do for you?" Rage said as he extended his hand to me.

"First, we are here to give you this." I handed him the notebook. "It is all the information I can give you about what happened to me."

Jasper took over from there. "Also, this morning this box was found on the door step at my house. We didn't open it. Mackenzie says the letters on the package are just like the ones from the envelope she received with the picture of the girl that started this whole mess."

Carefully Detective Rage took the box from Jasper. "Don't worry. We'll take care of this. Thank you for your help." He turned and started to walk away from us.

"Wait a minute detective. I want to know what's in there. It *is* addressed to me," I told him.

"If you would like to be involved in this we can arrange something, but only you and one other person. Not all of you can be in the investigation room."

"We'll wait here. We're not going anywhere. We'll be here when you get back." Charlotte rubbed my arm.

Rage led Jasper and I toward the back of the station. "Wait here," he said motioning toward an interrogation room. "I'll come back once the bomb squad clears the box."

We went into the room and sat down. For a few moments, we sat in silence. Before either of us had time to speak, Rage reentered the room.

"Where did you say that box came from?" Rage asked as soon as he joined us at the table.

"It was found at my front door," Jasper replied, only answering the question asked.

"Was there an address on the front when you found it?"

"No, it just had my name on the front, nothing else," I responded.

Rage's cell phone rang. "It's them. I'll be back." He left the room.

"What kind of suit are you planning to wear when we get married? Did you want to wear a tuxedo?" I asked Jasper as we waited.

"Isn't a tuxedo the traditional outfit for the groom?"

"Do you want our wedding to be traditional?"

"I want you to feel special. That is the only thing I want at our wedding." He smiled at me.

I leaned over and kissed his cheek. He put his hand on the back of my neck and pulled me to him. His mouth over took mine.

Detective Rage returned with the box in hand still unopened. "The bomb squad has determined the box is safe to open."

He placed the box on the table in front of me. I glanced over at Jasper who nodded at me in approval. I leaned over the box, but hesitated before opening it.

"Before you take anything out please put these gloves on in order to preserve any finger print evidence," Rage requested.

I obliged then reached in and the first thing I pulled out was a letter written ransom style with all the words cut from magazines. I shuddered just knowing this was a warning from 'The Butcher'.

"Hello Mackenzie, I want to tell you the story of the girl in the photos," I read aloud. I set down the letter, reached into the box and produced ten photos and a video tape then continued reading.

"She was Linda Blare. She had long chestnut brown hair. She was and has been the shortest of all at only four feet eight inches. I didn't even bother tying her to the chair like I did you." I wanted visual confirmation. I laid out the photos for everyone to see.

The first one was a visibly terrified, very alive Linda Blare clutching the arms of the exact same chair I had been held down to with duct tape. I continued, "To instill fear I lifted her out of the chair by grasping a handful of her hair at the back of her head. She screamed so loud I thought my eardrums would burst. I held her up over the blood stained concrete floor. She just hung there like a rag doll. She reached back and grabbed my wrist trying to lift herself up."

I consulted the next photo. The woman was on her hands and knees on the floor, clearly in pain. "I opened my hand and she fell onto her knees. When she tried to stand, I swung the baseball bat with a straight blow to her kneecap. She screamed in pain." I remembered how it felt when he had done that to me. I could feel a twinge of pain in my leg under the prosthetic where my actual leg now ended.

I glanced at the next picture where Linda was sitting on the floor leaning against the blood-splattered wall. Both of her legs fully extended out in front of her. I cringed as I continued.

"I chose a meat cleaver. I held it up over my head and brought it down with such force it chopped her leg completely off." The forth photo was Linda on the floor in the same spot her left leg was gone. Her eyes were wide with terror as blood spilled from the open wound.

"I remember blood gushing out as though a dam had busted. The video will show much more than the pictures.

Dear sweet Mackenzie, I hope you get the message. You were special. You were going to be my last, but you screwed that up. Everything I do from this point on is for you. If you want it to stop, you must give yourself up to me. I hope you enjoy the home movie enclosed. Remember, I am always watching you."

I spread out the other six photos. She is tied to the bed, blood everywhere. Then she is visibly dead, her eyes open and her body limp. He photographed her in the box and the box covered with a blanket. The last two pictures were of her grave. The first with the open hole, Linda was still in the box, but down in. The last was of the freshly covered grave.

I shoved all ten photos toward Detective Rage. He picked them all up and held them against his chest to cover the carnage.

"Why would he send this to me?" I asked.

"He said why in his letter. He feels like you screwed up his plan when you survived and this is his way of seeking revenge. He is showing you what he is capable of," Jasper answered.

"It was a rhetorical question honey, but thanks for the vote of confidence. He wants me to surrender to him or more bad things are going to happen." I wasn't crying this time. Apparently, the well had run dry.

"How did he know you were still alive and where you were staying?" Rage asked.

"It was announced on the news," I told him, irritated.

"How did the press find out? Who told them? Who did you tell you were staying at Jasper's house?"

"I told Charlotte and Jillian…" Rage cut me off.

"Besides them, who at the hospital did you tell?"

"Only Paul McConnell, my physical therapist and Doctor Morgan. Oh, and the nurse who found me and helped me emotionally, Claire."

"I am going to have to call them all in for questioning. The person who leaked this to the press could have ultimately put you and your friends in grave danger. I am going to set you up with an undercover police escort until we get this whole mess straightened out." Detective Rage put everything back in the box and walked Jasper and I back to the front of the police station.

Charlotte and Jillian stood when they spotted us coming. Rage called one of his undercover buddies to follow us home and watch the house all night. He told us we wouldn't even know he was there.

Thirteen

I was shocked at lunch on Wednesday when Malachi approached me at the diner and actually tried to have an unfeigned conversation with me. I felt uncomfortable and uneasy.

"Hey, how have you been doin'?" He asked as though we had been friends for years.

He wasn't as shy as he usually seemed. He was so weird and never really said anything worth listening to. I was trying to be pleasant without actually sounding awkward. He was just trying to be nice and I could see that, but having an actual conversation with him was a little bizarre.

"I'm recovering, thanks for asking."

"When he was holding you hostage, did he say anything to you that really frightened you?"

I wasn't sure if I wanted to answer the question, or why he even asked it in the first place, but I figured if I answered his questions maybe he would eventually go away. "He said we had been having a secret relationship and because I started dating Jasper it made him angry and that is the only reason he came after me."

"It sounds like you're in the middle of a forbidden affair. If this guy…" Malachi began.

"Psycho," I interrupted.

"Okay," he continued through gritted teeth. "If he thinks the two of you are in a relationship, my recommendation is to let Jasper go. You could inevitably be putting him in ultimate danger. Get as far away from him until your 'lover'," he motioned quotes with his fingers on both sides of his head, then continued, "has moved on." He spoke angrily, but with a smile. Patting me on the back, he awkwardly stroked my hair. He leaned in close enough to smell it. I could hear him taking deep breaths behind me.

I couldn't move, or think straight. I felt relief when Charlotte spoke up. She must have noticed the uncomfortable look on my face.

"Hey Malachi, could you get Jean so we could order?"

He squeezed my shoulder, hard, before walking away. I winced in pain.

"What the hell was that about?" Jillian asked leaning toward me to be discreet.

"That was way different than how he usually is," I said.

"That was way creepier than how he usually is," Jillian retorted.

"Anyway, let's just enjoy our lunch and each other's company. Charlotte you sure are being quiet."

"I'm sorry. I was just thinking about what Malachi said about Jasper being in danger. Maybe you should stay with one of us until this guy is caught." Charlotte touched my hand.

"I'm fine at Jasper's. I don't need you to baby sit me." I stood to leave but Charlotte tightened her grip on my hand.

"I am telling you if you continue to stay with Jasper something will happen to one or both of you."

I jerked my hand away from her. "You just don't want me to be happy. You have always wanted a better life than everyone else around you. Now that my life is better than yours, you want to take that away from me? I don't think so. I'm out of here." I walked as fast as my muscles would allow.

Once I was outside I realized I had rode with Jillian and I wasn't about to go back in. I leaned against the front fender of her car and waited. It didn't take long for her to join me.

"You were a little hard on her in there," Jillian said once we were in the vehicle and headed back to Jasper's house.

"She wants to ruin my perfect life. I have the perfect man and within a few months I will have the perfect family," I huffed.

"I could hardly call your life perfect. Do you not remember what you just went through? You do know how you got that baby for your perfect family, don't you? Seriously Mackenzie you should really apologize to Charlotte." Jillian always knew how to make me feel guilty.

I looked down at my fake leg and rubbed my abdomen. I didn't know what else to say. The rest of the car ride was in silence.

Once I had arrived back at Jasper's house I decided to sit out on the back patio to enjoy the weather. It was a beautiful Wednesday afternoon. It was approximately seventy-six degrees out with a cool northerly breeze.

I sat looking out at all the stunning spring flowers blooming as I clutched my cell phone. I was trying to figure out what I would say to Charlotte to apologize for what happened at lunch. So far all I had was, 'I'm sorry'. I looked down at the phone. Just before I began to dial, it rang.

"Hello," I answered.

"Mrs. Leigh, this is Detective Rage. I was wondering if you could come to the station to answer a few questions."

"Right now?"

"As soon as you can. There were letters on the back of the photos found in the box and I want to know if they mean anything to you."

"Jasper is at work until four and I haven't got that far in my physical therapy yet to be able to drive with my prosthetic."

"I'll be here late working on this case. I'll wait for you."

"I'll be there as soon as I can," I told him and hung up.

I quickly dialed Jasper and pressed the send button. "We need to go to the police station and visit with Detective Rage," I said as soon as he answered.

"Why? What happened?" Jasper asked with a worried tone in his voice.

"He called and said there was something we missed from the package."

"I'm on my way."

"Don't rush home for this. Rage said he was going to be working late and that he would wait for me."

"The sooner we get this taken care of, the sooner they can catch this guy." The line went dead.

I went inside and gathered some things to take with me. I decided I would call Charlotte later to apologize. Jasper arrived within a half hour and honked his horn from the driveway without even coming inside. I attempted a run but wasn't ready for that yet. I slowed down to a pace that was comfortable and headed out to Jasper in the awaiting vehicle. He drove straight to the police station and I told him about what happened at lunch.

"I think Jillian is right. You really should apologize to Charlotte as soon as we get home."

"What about what she said to me? She told me I should leave you." I grazed my fingertips over his cheek.

"That's not what it sounded like to me. It sounds like she is worried about you and thinks you would be in less danger if this maniac thought we weren't together anymore."

"No matter where I live, he isn't going to stop until I am dead."

I sat in silence and let his explanation mull around in my head. 'Maybe he's right,' I thought. 'But I don't want to be away from Jasper. He is what keeps me going.' I again rubbed my abdomen thinking I could feel the baby moving around.

When we arrived and stepped up to the desk the officer just waved us right in. We went straight back to Detective Rage's desk. He had the photos spread out and each one of the letters from the back of the pictures written on a dry erase board behind him.

"Mrs. Leigh, I wasn't expecting you so soon. Mr. Tully," he shook Jasper's hand. "These are the letters found on the back of each photo. Can you tell me if they mean anything to you?"

I looked at the letters written on the board. T, A, O, M, W, L, N, A, S, C were scrawled in red marker. I glanced over each letter carefully and nothing came to mind. I gave it a few minutes thinking that maybe if I stare at it long enough the answer would come to me.

I would shake my head after staring at a letter for five minutes each, then it hit me. "Maybe they are the first initial in a victim's name."

"What makes you say that?" Rage asked.

"Well, there is an M. My name is Mackenzie. The woman in the photos, he said her name was Linda. Hence the L." I circled each letter in green as I referenced them.

"I will go through all the victims that we know of then hit the missing persons list to see if I find anything. Is there anything else, you can think of that these letters might mean? Maybe he is trying to tell you who he is and all you have to do are unscramble the letters to get his name."

"I can't think of anyone with those letters. I have tried and tried to decode the letters, but nothing," I said.

"Here, have a look at some of these mug shots and see if you recognize any facial features, eyes, lips anything. Also, I want you to see if any of the names seem to match the letters." Rage handed me a thick binder full of photos of people who had been in prison at some point in their lives.

I placed one hand under the eyes and the other on the forehead trying to single out the one thing I stared at the most when I was being tortured. None of them looked familiar. None of the names matched all of the letters of the criminals. Some of their eyes were evil and others just looked like junkies. My hands were shaking as I flipped through the pages.

"I'm sorry, none of them look familiar, nor do any of their names match all of the letters up there on the board."

"If you think of anything to go with the letters please call and let me know," Rage said as he walked us out.

Jasper and I drove home discussing the possibilities.

"I agree with your idea about the victim's initials. I'm not so sure it could be as easy as the killer giving up his name. That sounds like someone who wants to be caught. 'The Butcher' doesn't seem like someone who wants to be caught," Jasper said.

"There is no possible way they are letters from his name. There is one thing he said to me that would confirm he would never give up his identity. He said, 'You are my last. Once I am done with you, I will disappear and in a few months no one will even remember who I am'. That doesn't sound like someone willing to give themselves up."

Fourteen

The next day I finally called to apologize to Charlotte. I sat on the bed in order to have some privacy. She didn't answer so I left her a voice mail to call me back. Before I had finished, my call waiting beeped in.

"Ms. Leigh? This is Detective Rage. I need you to stop by the station. We are bringing in Doctor Morgan, Paul McConnell and Claire Hussy for questioning."

"What do you need me there for?" I asked.

"I was hoping you would be willing to sit in on the interrogations and take notes confirming or contradicting their answers."

"I'm just going to sit in the room? Won't they wonder why I'm there?"

"They won't even know you're there."

"I'll be right over. Thank you Detective." I hung up the phone and went out to the living room where Jasper sat on the sofa thumbing through a wedding magazine.

"Did you get to talk to Charlotte?" He asked.

"No she didn't answer. Detective Rage called." I recalled the phone conversation for Jasper.

"Well, let's go," he said heading out to the car.

I followed behind. Once we were in the car Jasper started talking.

"I have been trying all morning to unscramble those letters and haven't come up with anything. Either there aren't enough letters or that wasn't his intended purpose."

"I told you I thought they were the first initials of his victims, not letters from his name. That theory just doesn't make sense," I supposed.

"I don't know. Maybe it is a message of some kind. Maybe there is more to it. There has to be more he just hasn't sent yet."

"Let's hope he doesn't send the rest of it. I don't want to know what he has to say."

We arrived at the station just in time to see Rage running to the front desk. "Who sent this? Where did this come from?" He yelled at the uniformed officer behind the counter.

"I don't know sir. It was on the desk when I came in this morning. It had your name on it so I took it to your desk."

Rage huffed then noticed Jasper and I standing there. "Come with me," he instructed.

We followed him into a room. He motioned for us to have a seat then threw a brown envelope down on the table in front of us. I reached for it and spilled out the contents. Four photos of me were sprawled on the table. I turned them over to reveal the letters I, H, N, I.

I flipped them back over to see two pictures of *me* on the bed. One with my leg still intact but my face was bloody and swollen. The other, my leg was missing and blood was gushing from the site of amputation. The other two were me tied to the chair. The first was of me knocked out when I first got there. I was still clean with no blood and my face was clear of all wounds. The second was after he had beaten me a few times. My eye was swelled shut, my nose was bleeding and there was blood running down my chin from my mouth.

"What the hell is going on here?" Rage asked.

"How am I supposed to know? These are pictures of *me*. Did you look into the missing person's reports for victims with their first initial matching the letters?"

"We tried your theory. There was a snag in the plan," Rage explained.

"What's that?" I asked.

"Not all of the victims have a letter to match their name and not all of the letters match a victim." Rage tossed a legal sized note pad on the table.

I flipped through about twelve pages worth of letters and names. Three pages where of him trying to unscramble the letters to make a name. None of it worked.

"What do we do now with these four extra letters?" Jasper asked.

"Nothing, absolutely nothing. He is just fucking with our heads. He is trying to distract us while he plans his next move. Come with me to the room next door so you can watch on the other side of the mirror." He led us out of the interrogation room and into a smaller room behind a door marked 'Private'.

There were three chairs placed directly in front of the two-way mirror. On our side, we could see directly into the empty interrogation room.

"None of them will be able to see you. Take this." Rage handed me three pens. "If you find any discrepancies in any of their answers, or if you have any additional comments, please write it down. This is the sound box. You will be able to hear everything."

Doctor Morgan was the first to go in for questioning. He came in and sat down facing the mirror. His expression was confused, but also frightened. Rage followed him in and sat across the table from him. At first, they just sat there, staring at each other silently.

"What is this all about? I have patients to attend to." Morgan spoke first.

"What kind of doctor are you?" Rage asked inquisitively.

"I'm an after care physician, why?"

"Who do you talk to about the patients in your care?"

"Only hospital staff who is also caring for that patient."

"Like who?" Rage questioned.

"Nurses, surgeons, physical therapists, nutritionists and the like. Depending on the needs of the patient."

"You don't talk to anyone outside of the hospital?"

"There is never any need to. I get patient permission before discussing their condition with family members unless the patient is unconscious, in which case the family is in control of the proper care of said patient."

"Has anyone ever posed as hospital staff to gain information on a patient that you may have inadvertently told personal information to?"

"Depending on the patient and their needs depends on whether or not I discuss any type of medical information with anyone. If I do, it is a trust worthy group of senior doctors and nurses with whom I have known for quite some time and are directly caring for the patient. I would never put any patient in danger."

"So your telling me you have no idea how the media could have got a hold of the information about Mackenzie Leigh?"

"I know better than to talk to reporters. They only report what they feel is *entertaining* they don't report the news." Morgan almost sounded irritated.

"Thank you for your time doctor. If you could just go back out to the front waiting area, I will let you know when you can go." Rage's tone sounded as though he felt belittled.

Before leaving the room, Rage passed by the mirror and shrugged his shoulders.

"I don't think Doctor Morgan is involved in any way. He sounded genuine when he talked about how he treats his patients," Jasper said as we waited for Rage to return.

"I never had any problems with him. He always treated me with the utmost respect," I replied.

When Rage returned, Paul was with him this time. I didn't think it could be Paul either. He was so sweet and helpful.

'Why would he try to ruin my life?' I thought.

"Who do you talk to about the progress of the patients you are helping?" Rage began.

"I only talk to authorized hospital personnel who is directly caring for the patient," Paul uttered.

"You don't talk to anyone outside the hospital?"

"Never. It is against hospital regulations to discuss a patient outside the care facility."

"You have never talked to anyone about a patient even if they are being unruly and you are just looking for someone to vent your emotions to?"

"What are you getting at detective? I haven't done anything wrong." Paul stood his ground.

"Who all did you discuss with the well-being of Mackenzie Leigh?"

"If you must know, I talked to Doctor Morgan, Nurse Claire, Doctor Kimball and Ma... myself. Yep, that's it, Doctor Morgan, Nurse Claire, Doctor Kimball and myself. Sometimes I like to talk out loud to myself about the patients I'm treating. Usually what got them there, how their progress is going, stuff like that." He looked around nervously as though he knew he had just dug himself into a slight hole he was going to have to be cunning to climb his way out of.

I jotted down the slip. The news anchorwoman who first announced my survival to the world was Marie Carter. I wrote that down too. I also noted his ridiculous explanation and the way he fidgeted in his seat when he repeated who he had talked to.

"Thank you Mr. McConnell. Please wait out front and I will let you know when you are free to go." Rage sounded more confident in his tone with Paul.

This time when he passed by the mirror he nodded his head.

"Did you catch that?" Jasper asked.

"I sure did. I made note of it. It is actually quite upsetting to think Paul was the one who could have potentially placed me right back into the hands of 'The Butcher'." I raised my eyebrows.

A few moments later, Rage returned with Claire. She appeared to be nervous. She was biting her fingernails and looking around like a skittish dog.

Detective Rage slammed a file down on the table, which made Claire jump. He pulled out a couple of pictures and placed them in front of her.

"Do you know who this is?" He asked.

"Of course, it's Mackenzie. Where did you get these?" She asked in an interested tone rather than being genuinely curious. I noted the tone.

"These were sent to the police station after someone had leaked information to the media about her survival. Do you know anything about that?"

"No, I didn't do it. I don't talk to anyone who could harm a patient of the hospital in any way."

"Do you ever discuss patients from the hospital with any one other than hospital personnel?"

"My sister sometimes, why?"

"Do you realize the danger some of those patients face if the wrong person gets a hold of certain personal information about them? Say for instance, a patient has survived an attempted murder from a serial killer. The killer thinks that she's dead. Problem is someone's big mouth announced it to a news reporter and the patient's life is now in danger." Rage was fuming.

"I'm sorry; I always make sure nothing too personal is told making sure not to put anyone in danger."

"Do you have any idea how the media could have become aware of that information?"

"It wasn't me. I promise, my sister wouldn't tell anyone either," Claire pleaded.

"How can you be sure? Where does your sister work?"

"She works for a funeral home. I'm sure the only people she talks to are dead. Did I do something illegal?"

"That is what we are trying to figure out. Please go back out to the front waiting area. I will let you know when you can go." Rage held the door open for Claire then joined Jasper and I in the small room on the other side of the two-way mirror.

"Did you figure out who it might be?" I asked.

"I am hoping your notes will help me come to that conclusion. I have an idea of who it could be, but I'm sure Doctor Morgan is clear," Rage confirmed.

"Doctor Morgan sounded sincere. I don't think he spoke to anyone," I said.

"I felt that Paul was about to reveal the name of someone that could have potentially led to the media. Claire said she talks to her sister who could leak to the press or be the press." I handed Rage the notepad.

"I'm going to tell Morgan he can go and call Paul to come back in for a few more questions. You can go ahead and go. I will call you when anything is exposed."

Fifteen

I walked through the trees easing branches out of my way as I approached the small shack. I didn't know how I had got there, but I knew I was there for a reason. The shack was just four small walls made up of mud and tree trunks. The wood had termite holes, or possibly a carpenter ant problem and rotting spots.

I stepped up to the one and only window and peered inside. It had only one room. In that room was a cot, a table and everything related to a kitchen. The table was packed with old, dirty jars.

I stepped around the porch to the front door. It was a lone screen door. I pulled it open. The rusty spring hinge screeched as it pulled apart then closed back together.

I slowly explored the confined area. It was dusty and smelled of rotting vegetables. The place made me feel dirty. I meandered through the shack, careful of everything I touched. I picked up a jar and examined it. It was full of a brownish liquid. It may have been clear once, but over time it changed color. I couldn't tell what was floating in it, then I realized I didn't really want to know. I replaced the jar back to the same spot from where I had lifted it.

There weren't any doors, other than the front door, that led to any other rooms, at least none that I saw. I stepped over near the cot and tripped on something bolted to the floor. I crouched down to touch it only to realize it was some kind of handle.

I shoved the cot out of the way. Pulling up on the handle, I realized it was attached to a hatch that was heavy and creaky. I pulled it all the way up then pushed it over in the opposite direction to reveal a large gaping hole in the floor. A flight of stairs manufactured out of six two inch by twelve inch pieces of plywood led down into a room underground.

I began my decent down to a dimly lit man made concrete room. The room seemed to be the source of the smell. It was rank and caused my nose to crinkle. When I reached the bottom of the steps, I spotted a chair. It was the same chair I had been tied to and tortured. I stepped up to the chair and saw Charlotte duct taped and unconscious.

I tried to release her, but my fingers couldn't grasp the tape. I freaked and kept scratching at the tape. I tried to scream, but my voice didn't work. As I dug my fingers into Charlotte's binding, the tips of all eight of my fingers began to bleed.

I grabbed her by the shoulders and shook her, in an attempt to wake her up. She wouldn't open her eyes and her body remained limp. I heard a noise up stairs. The rusty spring screeched, the screen door banged as it slammed shut. I could hear heavy footsteps walking toward the hatch.

I quickly scanned the room looking for another way out. I saw a small slit of light shining through another wooden hatch - there weren't any steps up to it, but I figured I could pull myself up through. Luckily, there was a table standing off to the left of it. I ran over and pushed it under the hatch. I hoisted myself up onto it. It wobbled and swayed back and forth under my weight.

I stood up, pushed open the hatch and pulled myself up. I was able to get my head, my arms and most of my body through. All that was left to pull through was from my hips down.

I was able to pull myself up far enough to sit on the ground outside. I could smell the fresh air. I had just lifted one leg out and began to stand when I felt something grab my ankle that was still inside. All of a sudden, I was yanked back in through the hole in the ground.

In the quick second it took him to jerk me through, I smacked my forehead on the wooden frame around the hatch. To make matters worse, I also banged the back of my head on the table. My back hit the ground with a deafening thud. I could see black spots in my line of sight, but I knew by the way this man was dressed he *was* 'The Butcher'.

He stood over me with a large chopping knife in one hand. I rubbed the back of my head as he lifted the knife up over his head. Before he could bring it down, I was able to bring up one leg. I kicked him as hard as I could in his stomach. He stumbled backward. I struggled to stand and ran over to where Charlotte was still strapped down. She was still unconscious and unmoving. I shook her again with no response.

'The Butcher' ran toward me with the chopping knife lifted over his head. I moved out of the way as he brought it down. It was plunged into Charlotte's stomach. I tried to scream again, but my voice was stifled as though someone were choking me.

I turned and ran up the stairs. His footsteps were heavy and loud behind me. I shoved open the screen door and continued to run, without looking back. I didn't need to. I could hear his footsteps and heavy breathing so clear as though I were listening to it through headphones.

It was now dark and foggy outside. As I ran, I tried to remember what trees I had seen when I was walking toward the house. He was getting closer. My feet were beginning to feel like I was wearing cinder block shoes, my legs like rubber. I could hear him breathing right behind me. I tripped on a tree stump and fell face first into a pile of leaves. I turned over so I was on my back and face to face with the maniac.

There he was, knife gripped tightly up over his head, standing over me. I couldn't move, could barely breathe. He brought his arms down. Just as the steel of the blade plunged down into my chest, I woke up, screaming. I sprung straight up covered in sweat and hyperventilating.

Jasper sat up in the bed next to me and wrapped his arms around my shoulders. He rocked back and forth attempting to comfort me. As the details of the dream replayed in my head, I realized Charlotte hadn't called me back yet so I could apologize.

"Something's wrong," I told Jasper as I grabbed my crutches and climbed out of bed.

"What is it sweetheart?" He asked leaning over my side of the bed to grab my hand.

"It was Charlotte in my dream. She died and…" I was crying as I told him about the horrible nightmare. "She must be in some kind of danger. She hasn't called me back yet. I have already left her two messages and if she hasn't returned my call by now, something must be wrong."

"Your subconscious mind is playing with you because you feel guilty. Come on, Mackenzie come back to bed. You have a doctor's appointment in a few hours and you need to sleep. You will see Charlotte tonight at dinner. Don't worry about it so much."

"She has never been this mad at me before. Even in high school when I read her diary. I would apologize to her the next day and we would be hanging out together that night. She forgave me, always. Something has to be wrong. She must be in danger."

"First of all, this isn't high school. This is real life. You're both grown up. Besides that, don't you think that if something were actually wrong with Charlotte, in that way, Tom would have called you by now to check if you've seen her?" Jasper raised his eyebrows and tugged a little on my hand.

I went ahead and rejoined him in the bed. "Maybe your right. If there really was something wrong with Charlotte, her husband would have called by now. Or at least Jillian would have. I'll wait until after my doctor's appointment to call her."

"Good, now let's go back to sleep." He kissed me on the forehead then cuddled in for the next few hours.

I couldn't get back to sleep. After each nightmare, I always just laid in bed wide-awake waiting for morning to come. Well not that time. I waited until I heard Jasper's breathing even out. I strapped on my leg and went out to the kitchen to make coffee.

I ate a couple of poached eggs, had two cups of coffee and did a little housework. I wandered around some – still trying to get use to walking with a leg I wasn't born with.

The sun was starting to rise and I knew Jasper would be up soon so I headed back to the bedroom to shower. As I was struggling to get out of the tub, he was heading into the bathroom to brush his teeth.

"Hey honey. Couldn't get back to sleep again?" He asked.

"No. You know how I get after those nightmares." I got dressed and ready for the day.

"That's why I think you should talk to someone."

I waved my hand at him in a fashion to tell him, 'I know, I know' and hoped he would drop the subject. We walked together out to the kitchen. He poured himself a cup of coffee while I packed some notes I had taken hearing other people talk about their pregnancy's, along with some questions to ask the doctor, into my purse.

I was still worried about Charlotte, but I figured no phone call was better than a worried one from Tom. I gripped my cell phone so tight on the way to the doctor's office I thought it would break.

Sixteen

We were halfway to our destination when my phone actually rang. The sound of the ring tone indicated it wasn't Charlotte. I almost didn't want to answer it.

"Hello," I said glumly.

"Well Mrs. Leigh. I would think you should sound a lot happier to know we have someone in custody," Detective Rage's voice spoke through the earpiece.

"You caught 'The Butcher'?" I asked excitedly.

Jasper pulled over and stopped the car. He watched me, hoping for the answer we had been waiting for.

"Well now, let's not get ahead of ourselves. That's not what I said," Rage replied.

"Then what are you talking about?" I shook my head and waived my hand motioning for him to continue driving.

"We were able to get a confession out of Paul McConnell. He was the one who talked to the media."

"What did he say in his confession? Why did he do this to me?" I demanded.

"He said it was because he has a crush on you. He figured if you saw the news report and thought you were in danger you would leave Jasper."

"Then what? I would just go running into *his* arms like a scared little girl. I don't think so. What about the pictures and the package? Did he say anything about that?" I didn't know what I was going to do about a physical therapist now.

"He said he didn't have anything to do with that. He swore up and down he never meant to hurt you."

"Do you believe that, Detective?" I asked.

"I actually do. He sounded sincere enough. He even cried a little."

"Thank you, Detective. Please keep me informed."

"Will do."

I hung up the phone and relayed the conversation to Jasper.

"Think of it this way, that's one down and one to go," he said in his attempt to comfort me.

"The one down just has a big mouth. The one to go TRIED TO KILL ME!" I yelled, crying.

"Alright, I'm sorry. I'm just trying to help." He continued to the doctor's office, pouting.

When he parked the car, I turned toward him and touched his arm. "I'm sorry. It must be these pregnancy hormones. I don't mean to get snappy. It just kind of happens. I love you."

"I love you too, Mac."

The way he shortened my name made me freeze in my seat. I literally could not move. "What did you just call me?" I stared straight out the windshield without looking over at him.

There was only one person in my whole life who ever called me that. "I called you Mac. That is still okay, right?" He asked.

When I was in the sixth grade and living with my seventh foster family, there was only one person who lived in the house with me that I felt a strong connection with. His name was Jojo. Every time I would ask him what his last name was, he always told me he didn't have one like Cher, or Madonna, or Prince. I just called him Jojo and he always called me Mac.

He was a sweet, but challenging boy. He had manners, always said ma'am and sir, but would sneak out of the house at night when we were supposed to be in bed.

The foster parents we were staying with decided, after six months, they could no longer handle him. There was a family who would adopt foster children that were on the wrong path in life and try to change their lives.

He may have been two years older than me, but I loved him and I knew he loved me too. The family that adopted him had made the decision years ago to home school their children due to thinking that public school is what corrupted the child's mind. I was devastated when he left the foster home. For two years afterward, I bounced around from group home to group home, intentionally being kicked out of each one after only a few weeks hoping I would see him again.

I stopped moving around when I got to the home with Charlotte and Jillian and their adoptive parents decided not to give up on me.

I was happy to have a permanent home, but was always thinking about Jojo. Now here he was, right under my nose the whole time and I never even noticed.

The face he made and the tone in his voice I knew it was him. "Jojo? Is it you? Is it really you?" Tears welled up in my eyes.

He got out of the car and came around to my side. He opened the passenger side door for me, held out his hand like a gentleman to help me out of the car. Once we were face to face, I looked deep into his eyes and wondered why I didn't see him in there before. I softly touched his cheek and ran my fingertips around the shape of his mouth.

"It's me. It's always been me. When I spotted you from across the diner, I felt that spark. The same connection we had all those years ago. I didn't know how you felt about me then. I wanted to wait to reveal my true identity to you when I knew you felt the same way about me as I do and always have about you."

I was overjoyed. "I thought I would never see you again. Yet here you are, posing as some guy named Jasper Tully when all this time you could have told me who you were and we would be going to see the doctor today because I was carrying your baby instead because of some crazed lunatic who was having a secret relationship with me." I wrapped my arms around his neck and hugged him, hard, even though I was mad at him.

"Actually Mac, my real name *is* Jasper Tully. When I was younger, I just thought Jojo made me sound cool. I am still the same person you have always known and have come to know."

"I can't believe you didn't tell me. I'm mad at you. I still love you, I always have, but I'm mad at you for not telling me it was you." I pulled him in close to me again and he wrapped his arms around my waist.

I pressed my lips against his. His mouth took over mine until I remembered where we were and pulled back.

Seventeen

Together we sauntered into the doctor's office. Walking up to the window, signing in, I joined Jasper at the row of chairs in the waiting area. It was only a few minutes before I was called in to see the doctor.

The nurse took me back, Jasper followed.

"Step up onto the scale and we will see how much weight you have gained," the nurse told me.

"Hopefully it's not too much," I said.

"Considering you are approximately five months along you should have gained at least ten pounds. It's not too bad. This is only your first. With my first I lost all the weight within the first three months after he was born, it was the second and third pregnancy I haven't been able to lose all the weight from."

"Oh, that's comforting." I stepped up on the scale and watched as she moved the larger balance to the one hundred mark and moved the smaller balance down... down... down to the fifty mark. I lowered my head, looking at my slightly protruding belly and realizing all the gain was out front.

"Alright, now you are going to take this into that bathroom," she said, handing me a specimen cup to urinate in. "Then when you are finished the doctor will meet you in exam room three," the nurse told me motioning down the hallway to a brown door with an oversized 3-dimensional green number three nailed to the door.

Jasper waited for me outside the bathroom door then escorted me to the exam room.

The room was only fifteen feet by fifteen feet. There was a counter with a sink in the middle and cabinets underneath. A paper-lined bed was positioned caddie corner with the head to the right of the door. There were two chairs. One was a stool type on wheels, the other a regular armchair. Jasper chose the armchair as I pulled myself up and sat on the paper-lined bed.

"I guess this is it, the moment of truth," Jasper said shrugging.

We didn't wait long before the doctor came in with the same nurse who told us to wait. The obstetrician was holding a hand held radio device with a microphone type attachment.

"Would you like to hear your baby's heartbeat?" She asked.

Jasper stood up and walked over to hold my hand. She placed the microphone on my abdomen after squeezing a jelly type lubricant on the tip. After a couple of seconds of wind noise excreting from the hand held speaker box as she rolled the microphone over my belly, came a quick whooshing sound.

Whoosh, whoosh, whoosh…

"Do you hear that? That is the sound of the baby's heartbeat. Wait a minute, what's this?" She got a puzzled look on her face as she moved the fetal heart monitor around to another spot. Suddenly there were two separate whooshing sounds and the doctor's expression changed to elation.

Whoosh, whoosh…whoosh, whoosh…whoosh, whoosh

"Have the two of you ever thought of the possibility of twins?"

I began wondering if maybe we should have told her how I came to be expecting. I withheld that information because I didn't want her pity. I didn't want to be the one who every time I came in she asked if I was holding up okay. Everyone in the hospital asked me that question every damn day and I was tired of it. No one really understands. I am trying to be so strong and get over the tragedy of what happened. The more times and the more people who ask if I'm okay will result in a complete break down.

"No, no way. Check it again. Do another test. This can't be happening." I gripped Jasper's hand so tight I thought I heard him whimper.

"I could do an ultrasound and you could see for yourself. Sara, could you escort them to the sonogram room," She told the nurse.

The doctor left and we were escorted to another room. There was the same kind of paper-lined bed, but there was also a giant machine with a television screen, sporadic buttons and a rolling ball like you would see on a *Golden Tee* arcade golf game.

The nurse explained to the technician what she was to be looking for then left the room. The tech squeezed more of the lubricant onto my abdomen, turned on the screen, picked up the transducer and placed it in the same general area the doctor had. Since the machine was practically behind me, there was another large television screen in front of me mounted to the wall.

I watched as she navigated my uterus and pointed out two small black specks on the screen. She said the two blobs were my babies. She measured both of them then printed out a couple of pictures from different angles. Handing me the printouts, the technician wiped the gel substance off my belly and told me the doctor would like to see me in her office.

We sauntered down the hallway to the office area and sat in two chairs strategically placed in front of a desk. As Jasper and I waited for the doctor to join us, I cried. Not only was I pregnant as the result of rape, but now I was going to be having two of the maniac's babies. I was sure, at this point, I was being punished for something I had done.

"Are there any questions, comments, concerns? Anything you may want or need to ask? Don't worry, there are no stupid questions. Trust me, I've heard them all," the doctor said when she finally joined us.

"I can't even wrap my head around the concept of twins. I know I have been eating a lot more than normal, but I just figured it was a pregnancy thing. I didn't realize I was eating for three," I commented.

"Technically you are still only eating for one. Don't over stuff yourself. The best meal plan is instead of eating three large meals a day you should really be eating about six small meals. You are still feeding the babies, but just a little at a time rather than starving them for hours before stuffing yourself silly. The babies will only take in a little at a time anyway." The obstetrician handed me a book to help me understand the changes my body would be going through over the next few months.

I scanned it. "Thank you for all your help," I said as we stood to leave.

"I am going to need to see you again next month. I look forward to navigating you through this special time in your life. Please stop and make an appointment with the nurse on your way out," she explained.

Jasper and I walked quietly out to the car. I cried all the way back to his house. All I could do was stare at the ultrasound picture of the two unwanted babies growing inside my body.

Eighteen

Even though Charlotte never called me back to allow me to apologize, she was at dinner Friday night.

"Charlotte, I am so sorry I over reacted on Wednesday. I really didn't mean any of it. I think it was just the hormones." I hugged her. "I was so worried." Tears formed in my eyes.

"I accept your apology. I would like to apologize myself for causing you to worry. I didn't realize how upset I made you when I didn't call you back." We hugged again then sat down to enjoy our meals.

"So, Jasper, how is everything going at home?" Jillian asked.

I sighed heavily knowing what was coming next.

"Mackenzie has been having severe nightmares, almost every night," he said, running his hand across my back from shoulder to shoulder.

I sat quietly, eating, waiting for my opportunity to jump in and explain my side, knowing what Jasper was getting at.

"Nightmares? What are the nightmares about?" Charlotte asked, as though she were inquiring about a child.

"Usually, she is reliving the kidnapping and torture. Other dreams are almost like she is dreaming the future. There was one nightmare she had that included all the events that happened to her, only they were happening to Charlotte."

"Have you thought about taking her to go talk to someone?" Jillian asked.

At this point I'd had enough. "Okay, could the three of you please stop talking about me as though I'm not here? Jasper, I can't believe you trapped me in this mess. Like I told you numerous times before, I am not going to talk to someone who sits there, listening to me blab on and on about something that I would rather forget and then ask me, 'how did that make you feel'? I know how it made me feel. I didn't like it when it was happening to me and I don't like it when I have to relive it every night in my dreams. I would rather forget it happened and move on with my life. Now then, can we please either change the subject or just eat in silence. Thank you," I commented.

Once all six of us had leaned back in our chairs, proving we had eaten enough, I broke the news about the babies.

"How do you feel about that? You had just accepted the fact that you were going to have a baby. Are you happy or sad now that there are two?" Charlotte asked rubbing my arm.

"I'm a little indifferent. I have had several thoughts rolling around in my head. I don't understand why this had to happen to me. Think about it… First, I was raped which resulted in a pregnancy and now there is two of them growing inside me. What if one of them turns out to have the same murderous mentality?" Tears formed in my eyes, again.

"Are you really worried about how the babies will turn out or whether you will love them the same way if you had conceived them in love?" Jillian asked reaching over the table to affix my hair behind my ear.

I shrugged as I stared down at my hands and thought about how I really felt. *Would I really be happier if the ba-*

bies had been conceived under different circumstances? I thought.

"Come on, Honey. Let's go home," Jasper said as he helped me to my feet.

"Mackenzie, I hope all goes well for you," Tom told me when we had stepped out the front door of the diner.

"Thank you, Tom." I wrapped my arms around his neck in an embrace.

Mark placed his hand on my shoulder. "Don't worry, Kenz. We will all be here for you no matter what you decide or go through."

"That is so sweet, Mark. Ya'll are the best family a girl could have."

We were all quiet for a few minutes before saying our good-byes and going our separate ways. While Jasper drove home, I rubbed my abdomen and thought about the two small human beings living inside me.

"Are you okay?" Jasper asked as he pulled into the driveway.

"I guess. Sometimes I wish this would all just go away so we could start over." Tears blurred my vision.

"All what would go away?"

"The pregnancy, the babies. I wish there was someway to get rid of them naturally so we could start over and have our own baby. Does that make me a bad person?" Tears were now rolling down my cheeks.

"No, that doesn't make you a bad person. It just means you are scared and that is perfectly normal. Now let's go inside and plan our wedding. Would that make you feel better?" Jasper brushed the backs of his fingers over my cheek.

I nodded and we exited the vehicle. As we approached the front door, we both noticed the package in the same spot as the first. My name was pasted on the front in the same manor as the other. Jasper picked up the box, ushered me inside.

"We will deal with it in the morning," Jasper told me.

I nodded my head in agreement and we headed to the living room leaving the parcel on the table in the foyer.

"What colors do you like? I'm not that interested in red. It seems too traditional. I want something a little less traditional. This is not the most traditional setting. My life isn't exactly traditional." I raised my eyebrows and giggled as I pulled up my skirt to reveal my plastic leg.

"The colors are really up to you. You should choose your favorite color and incorporate that into the flowers. How about this setup?" He pointed at a picture, in one of the many wedding magazines we had purchased, of a flower arrangement made out of daisies, lilies and sunflowers.

It looked like a centerpiece and I wasn't sure how I would incorporate that into the bouquets. The sunflowers had long stems, not to mention they were big flowers to begin with. The daisies and lilies looked like they were only an attempt to tone down the sunflowers.

"I'm not so sure about the yellow. It is too close to white and it isn't really a fun color. I want a fun color. What do you think about a shade of purple? I was thinking maybe lavender or lilac. What do you think about those colors?"

"To tell you the truth honey, purple is purple to me. It doesn't matter how you lighten or darken the color it's all the same color to me." He looked deep into my eyes and smiled. "How about a little bit of blue and green? You could find flowers to accommodate that couldn't you?"

"I bet I could. That is totally non-traditional. We could see if we could get an arrangement of violets and bluebonnets. We could also mix it with a wonderful selection of emerald and jade leaves. This is going to be the most fantastic wedding ever." I smiled and hugged him.

"I'm not sure what shade of blue or green those are, but we could color coordinate the tuxedos and bridesmaid dresses to match. You could choose one color for the bridal party and the other color for your dress if you're not interested in a traditional white dress." He looked lovingly into my eyes and brushed his fingers across my cheek.

We leaned in toward each other. Passionately, hungrily, he took over my mouth with his. He lowered me down to the sofa and positioned his body on top of mine. I immediately began feeling uncomfortable and wanted to cry.

"Please stop. I can't do this, please," I cried out, pushing him away from me.

He sat up and assisted me back into an upright position. "I'm sorry. I know what you have been through. I allowed my hormones to take over. Please, forgive me."

I placed my hand on his chest over his heart. "What has happened to me is not your fault. I am still feeling a little violated. Knowing what he did to me while I was unconscious just makes me sick to my stomach. Unfortunately, now your touch makes me feel uncomfortable. With time and patience, I'm sure I will get over it."

"This is why I keep telling you to go talk to someone."

"And I keep telling you, I don't need to talk to anyone. I will get over it in my own way. Let's keep looking for wedding ideas and change the subject." I smiled at him, then grabbed another bridal magazine from the coffee table.

We continued thumbing through the magazines gathering color scheme ideas, but the entire time all I could think about was the box. I wanted to know what this one contained. How different or similar the contents were.

Jasper must have noticed the far away look in my eyes. "If you want to know what is in the box that bad just go get it. I'll clear this stuff."

He cleared the periodicals off the coffee table; I brought in the box and placed it in the center. We sat on the sofa and stared at it the same way we had the first one. I leaned forward and placed my hands, palms down, on top of the box as though I were trying to feel what was inside.

"Well, are you going to open it?" Jasper asked.

I turned my head to smile at him then turned back and pulled the tape off the top of the box, slowly. On top was the same type of ransom note. There were eleven photos and a video. I flipped the pictures over immediately without looking at the gruesome scenes captured on the front.

The letters this time were N, T, A, O, I, W, S, N, D, I, N. Jasper leaned forward, reaching his hands out as though he were going to move the pictures around.

"Wait," I said stopping him from touching anything. "The letters may not be in order, but the note tells the story of this woman in this order. You can move them around when I finish reading the letter."

He pulled his hands back and leaned into the couch. He looked as though he were waiting for me to read him a bed-time story. I held the note in both hands and began reading out loud.

"Dearest Mackenzie,

I hope you have taken serious thought to my last letter to you. I hope you plan to surrender to me. I will continue to communicate with you this way, but only until I can't wait any longer. After that my threats will become more violent until I have you again and finish what I started." I shuddered. I wasn't sure if it was out of fear or if this guy was just too creepy for me. Maybe it was a little of both.

I continued, *"This one is Nancy Marshal. She almost looked just like you. Her hair was the same, her eyes were the same, her face even had your bone structure. The main difference was her body. She didn't have the same sexy hourglass figure you have. Nancy was a fighter just like you were. I had to tie her down then tape her to the chair."*

I turned over the first picture. This woman appeared to have already been beaten. Her eye was purple and swollen; her nose was bloody and looked as though it had been broken. Her bottom lip was about three sizes larger than the top. She was strapped to the dental chair. Silver duct tape held her arms from her wrists to her elbows and her feet and ankles were taped to the extreme as well. I went back to the letter and kept reading.

"It wasn't easy to break her thumbs. I had to do it while she was tied down. To ensure she wouldn't run, I went ahead and broke her knee cap as well before transporting her to the bed."

The second picture was of Nancy's broken thumbs. Her hands hung limp over the arms of the chair and if I looked close enough I could see bone protruding where her thumb joint used to connect to her wrist.

I turned over the third photo. Now Nancy's head hung down. Her hands were in the same position. Her left leg was clearly broken. He must have been incredibly angry when he swung the bat. I could tell he had struck her more than once.

I continued reading, *"I cut the tape and the rope from her arms and legs, then pulled her out of the chair by her hair. As you may notice from the pictures she was already bleeding pretty badly."*

I turned over the fourth picture. She had cuts up and down her arms and legs where he had apparently used the knife to cut the tape. The rope was still tied around her wrists and ankles. Each cut was bleeding, profusely.

The fifth photo was Nancy still in the chair, but without the rope. It appeared as though he had slit her wrists and sliced her ankles. Blood was dripping from her body.

I hesitated before flipping over the sixth gruesome scene. I rubbed my eyes then looked over at Jasper. He looked anxious for me to finish as though he knew something I didn't. I turned it over just to see Nancy laying face down on the concrete floor.

"I dragged her to the bedroom by her hair – it was the only part of her I could get a good grip on. I almost didn't tie her to the headboard or footboard seeing as she had no fight left in her. I realized it wouldn't be much fun for me if I didn't."

The seventh photo showed Nancy, bloody and disheveled, tied to the bed. Her skin was almost a completely different color from all the blood. I placed the letter down in my lap and didn't know if I wanted to read the rest or see the last four snapshots. Knowing that there would be a message for me at the end of the note I kept reading.

"For Nancy I chose the machete. I lined it up just above her broken kneecap. Instead of chopping, I sawed. Back and forth and back and forth until it was no longer attached."

The eighth photo was her without her leg. A blood pool formed on the bed and floor. Her eyes were closed so there was no way of knowing if she were alive at that point.

"Remember Mackenzie, you are the only one who can make this stop. Surrender to me and no one will ever hear from me again. Prolonging the inevitable will only anger me and devastate others. It will also cause your death to be slow and painful. Yours truly, 'The Butcher'."

I turned over the last three photographs. They were identical to the last three of Linda's. Nancy in the box, the box in the grave with her in it covered with a blanket and the freshly covered grave.

I flipped the pictures back over and examined the letters. Jasper immediately began shuffling around the letters trying to create a word. The way he moved them was like three card Monty, sliding them around in circles and crossing them over each other.

"I think I figured it out. If I take these four and make one word, then take these seven, move this one here and there it is. Dina Townsin." He looked so proud of himself.

"How does that have any significance? Who's Dina Townsin?"

"She's the woman from years ago who's husband caught her cheating. He beat her then cut off her left leg and hung it in the dining room right over the table. They said once he knew she was dead, he took a twelve gauge shot gun, placed it in his mouth and blew his brains out."

"Why would 'The Butcher' send a message with her name on it?"

"Let's go find out. We can ask Rage if the letters from the other pictures connect somehow."

"We really should wait until morning," I said looking at the clock.

"Your right. Well what do we do until then? Do you want to watch the video?" Jasper smirked.

"Not at all. That's the last thing I want to do. Let's just go to bed. Morning always comes faster when you sleep."

Nineteen

When we arrived at the police station the next morning, I noticed an abundance of black vehicles with dark tinted windows. Every one of them had government issued license plates. Jasper and I both looked at each other wondering if they were there to help catch 'The Butcher'.

The atmosphere in the station was different from usual. There was more hustle and bustle than before. There were men and women wearing black suits everywhere. Everyone was working on something with a partner.

"Please, go right on back," we were told by the officer at the front desk.

We walked right through all the way to the back. The back wall was covered with pictures of women along with bios of each identified victim.

"What's going on?" I asked Rage as soon as we saw him.

"The FBI has decided to help us with the investigation and capture of 'The Butcher'. They are the behavioral analysis unit out of Quantico, criminal profilers. Based on certain similarities in each case, they can figure out where this person might work, how he grew up and his personality around people who are not his victims."

"What kind of profile have they come up with so far?"

"They have only reviewed these photos so far. They would like to talk to you before they make a final profile decision."

"Who are all these women," I asked pointing at the list.

"The notes under each picture tell why she is on the board. We started with Linda Blare. He openly admitted to killing her. Right now, we have officers out with the cadaver dogs trying to see if they can find her body. According to the missing persons report, all we may find are her bones. She's been missing for five years."

I walked along the wall looking for Nancy. "Detective, I know this one is a victim," I told him when I found her photo.

A note card under her image read *still missing*. I knew that wasn't true. I handed the letter and the photos of her to Rage. He reached up, pulled the pushpin out of the note card, flipped it over and pressed the pushpin back through the same hole in the card. The other side read *victim*.

"I think I have figured out the letter pattern he has been sending. Check this out." Jasper walked over to the dry erase board. It still contained the first set of letters along with the extra four sent later. "If you move the O and the W next to the T, take the N and put it after that, then go to the second set of letters and take an I and an N and put it after the S and put those together as one word," He wrote the new letters from Nancy's pictures on the board. "They match from both sets of photos and spell out Townsin. The extra letters here spell Dina. Isn't that what the news said that woman's name was whose husband had killed her?"

"Yes, it was. Do you remember what her husband's name was? Maybe that's the name in the first set of pictures. I'm sure we didn't see it before because it was incomplete. Now that we have all the letters and we know what this one says maybe we can figure it out," I said looking at the board.

"Once the news started talking about the similarities, we tried that. The letters aren't right. His name was Corbin.

There isn't a B in any of those letters, nor is there an R," Rage pointed out.

"Well, these seven letters spell Townsin. It has to be a family member. Did Dina and Corbin have any children?" Jasper asked.

"Let me get the file. I'll let you know." Rage walked away leaving us standing there staring at the board.

"Wait a minute. Look at this." Jasper wrote a name on the board, but blocked it with his body. "Keep an open mind."

He stepped aside. I couldn't believe what I was seeing. He had written Malachi Townsin. The letters matched, but it didn't make sense. *Why would Malachi try to hurt me? Could he have had an unhealthy obsession directed towards me?* I wondered.

"I know which Malachi you are referring to, but I'm not sure of his last name. That first name could have just been popular the decade from when he was born." I told Jasper.

"He is a creepy guy. This could have been what sent him over the edge. His parents died when he was young, he says weird and off the wall things. Don't you think this kind of explains some of the things he says?" Jasper analyzed.

Detective Rage returned with a manila file folder with the police stations seal on the front. "Dina and Corbin Townsin had a son," he read from the file. "His name was Malachi Townsin. The neighbor from across the street discovered their bodies when Dina didn't show up for their weekly girl's night. Apparently every Thursday night six women would get together away from their husbands and children and play games or gossip."

"Wait a minute. Do you mean Malachi, the manager from the diner my sisters and I frequent every Wednesday, could be the Townsin boy?" I asked.

"It is possible. It says here the neighbor mentioned the child, but he was never located. He *could* be the missing piece to the puzzle. He could either be 'The Butcher' or we are being warned that he could be the next victim." Rage closed the file and placed it on his desk.

"Incase you haven't noticed Detective, all the victims have been female. I think he is ready to be captured. Maybe in some small way he is giving himself up," Jasper remarked.

"Wait just a damn minute. Don't you think that sounds a little too easy?" I ranted.

"Maybe, but either the killer has identified himself or is attempting to frame an innocent man. I'll let the police know and have him picked up and brought in for questioning." Rage picked up his phone.

"Wait, I know what he is doing. He is giving up his identity to *me* so I can give myself up to him," I whispered to Jasper. "He has been sending these things to me personally. Whether he thought I would go to the police with it or not, he was trying to tell me who he was."

"So what are you going to do?" He asked.

"Try to get to him before they do." I turned and started walking toward the front.

Jasper grabbed my arm trying to stop me. "Don't do it Mac. You don't know what he is capable of."

"If I don't he will continue to send these packages to me and eventually he may end up hurting someone else. I don't want that someone else to end up being Jillian or Charlotte. Don't worry Jojo, I'll be careful." He let me go. He even handed me the keys to his car.

I leaned toward him and pecked him on the mouth. I wasn't sure how I was going to drive. I hadn't got that far in my therapy yet. I was sure as hell going to figure it out, fast.

Realizing driving was going to be easier than I thought, I slid in behind the wheel, used my own right leg to push the petals and took off down the street toward the diner.

Twenty

When I arrived, there was a sign on the front door that read *'Go around back'*. I pulled the sign down and followed the instructions. In the back was a large metal door. I pushed the door open and stepped in to an area the dumpster inhabited. The smell of old rotting food was causing my stomach to do summer saults on top of my heart beating at the speed of sound.

There was another door attached to a chain link fence. Turning the knob, I opened the door. I stepped up to the back door of the building. There was another note. It read *'Please ring bell for service'*.

How cliché, I thought, but pressed the button anyway to ring the bell. I looked around the little area I was practically trapped in, trying to find an escape hatch somewhere; just in case I needed a quick exit strategy.

When my back was to the door, it was opened so rapidly I didn't even see the person on the other side. Quickly I was grabbed and pulled in.

The door slammed shut. I was being held by someone I couldn't see. He was behind me with one arm around my waist and the other around my neck. He whispered in my ear, "Scream and I'll slit your throat."

I remained calm. "How did you know I would come?" I asked.

He dragged me to the manager's office and practically threw me into the chair, then closed the door. The office was so small it was claustrophobic with the two of us crammed in. He stood over me with a knife in his hand.

"Malachi, what did I ever do to you?" I asked.

"You never acknowledged my existence. I would sit every Wednesday and watch you. You would look over at me, I would smile and you would look away, disgusted. You always acted like I was beneath you. I would even come over to your table and talk to you. I could hear every word you ever said about me being creepy."

Surprisingly my breathing was slow and even. "How did you know I would come tonight?" I repeated.

"I knew once you received the second package with my mother's name scrambled on the photos you would come to me."

"Jasper put the letters together."

"Your boyfriend is a smart guy," Malachi said sarcastically as he ran his fingers through my hair.

I slapped his hand away. "Don't touch me."

The knife in his hand moved so quickly I hadn't even realized the blade had even grazed me until I felt the blood running down my cheek. I lifted my right hand to my cheekbone and touched the cut. The human biological oils excreted from my fingertips caused it to sting.

"You son of a bitch." I leaped from the chair at him.

He managed to catch me almost mid-air and held onto me as I struggled. I was going to get away from him again. I just kept telling myself, 'I am not a victim.'

I kicked and pushed my feet against the wall, shoving him backward into a type of built in desk. It was made out of the laminate counter top material, but with a notch cut out the length and width and had a thick piece of Plexiglas placed down into the notch.

"Owe, you better stop fighting it Mackenzie. I am going to kill you this time and trust me, I won't feel bad about it."

Grabbing a rope, Malachi hog tied me, carried me out the same door I came in, practically throwing me into the back seat of a vehicle.

I wiggled and squirmed just enough so I could reach my cell phone from my pocket. I pulled it out and called Jasper. Once it began ringing, I turned down the earpiece volume so Malachi wouldn't hear when Jasper answered. I placed it at the edge of the seat and slowly let it fall to the floor. Unfortunately, we were in an SUV and the seats were further from the floor than in a sedan. I cringed when I knew he heard the thud!

"What are you doing back there?" Malachi yelled.

"I'm sorry. It's not exactly comfortable back here tied up like this. Is there any way you could untie me?" I squirmed around banging different parts of my body against everything I could find back there, attempting to recreate the sound. Luckily, he took that explanation.

"Why? So you can try to escape or fight me? I know you would do anything to get away from me. I know you probably have some idea of what I am going to do with you."

I watched the timer on my cell count the duration of the phone call. I decided Jasper would need some information to know where he was taking me, so I began by asking questions.

"Where are you taking me, Malachi?"

"To a place you know all to well."

"We're going back to that stinky disgusting hell hole you apparently live in?"

"Better than that. Since I'm sure you have contacted the police about the presents I have been leaving for you, they are probably already at my house searching through my stuff. I have decided this time to go to where our journey began. Your house," he laughed as though he had told an incredibly funny joke.

I hadn't been there since my release from the hospital when Jasper tried to get me to go inside for some clothes. Considering I was already with the kidnapper, I figured there was no reason to be afraid of the house.

Twenty-one

When we arrived, he took my keys from my pocket and unlocked the front door then came back for me. He carried me in and sat me in the first chair in the living room.

"I see you have recovered nicely," he said as he removed the rope and my prosthetic leg.

"I see you're still psychotic."

He quickly slashed the knife across the other side of my face. I was hoping Jasper answered his phone and he was on his way to save me. I was also hoping he had thought to bring Detective Rage along. Maybe even the local police and the FBI.

"Your sassy mouth is gonna get you killed sooner. I was planning to play with you for a while. Are you ready to die Mackenzie?"

"I'm pregnant Malachi," I said as though it would make a difference.

"I can see that. What is that supposed to mean to me?"

"The doctors in the hospital told me you raped me."

"Honey, I didn't rape you. I consummated our relationship." He sounded as though he believed what he said.

"Well, thanks to that I am pregnant." I was trying to filter my fear into anger and frustration.

"You mean your gonna have my baby?" He actually sounded happy.

"More like babies. It's twins."

"That's even better." He looked up at the ceiling. "See momma. I told you I would make you some grandbabies some day. If one's a girl, I'll name her after you." He shifted his focus back to me.

"Like hell you get any say in what goes on with these babies. They're mine and you can't do anything to get them." I wrapped my arms around my stomach and pulled my only leg up in the chair.

"I'll get them and I'll have all the say. I could tie you up and wait for you to give birth then take them and disappear. These are my babies too even if I have to cut them out of you."

"That is the only way you're going to get these babies, you psycho." I hugged myself tighter.

"Now is that any way to talk to the father of your children?" He was practically nose to nose with me, so I spit in his face.

He placed the blade of the knife between his teeth. He sat on my knee until my foot was back on the floor. I leaned forward to shield my abdomen. He straddled me and grabbed my wrists. He was stronger than I was so he was able to pull my arms apart. No matter how much I struggled, he was still able to hold both wrists in one hand and up over my head. With his other hand, he removed the knife from his mouth.

I squirmed and kicked my right leg. I screamed hoping someone would hear me and come to my rescue. He sliced up my face a few more times telling me to shut up with every attack.

"Please don't hurt my babies. Please, please don't hurt my babies," I pleaded. I hadn't realized how much I cared for the babies until that moment.

He didn't listen to me. He cut up my arms until I stopped struggling. By then the only reason I ceased was due to lack of strength caused by blood loss. I could feel the blood dripping off my face and trickling down my arms from each individual cut.

"Please Malachi. You don't want to do this," I cried.

"I want those babies more than you do." There was an anger and determination in his eyes I had never seen before.

He gently placed the blade across my abdomen. With surgeon like precision, he cut across from hip to hip. I screamed out with excruciating pain radiating throughout my entire body. I could feel the warm crimson liquid flowing from my lower torso and soaking my pants. It felt as though I had wet myself. Of course, I may have wet my pants without even knowing it.

Just before the knife made its second entrance into my body, the front door was blasted open. Approximately twenty to thirty police officers, FBI agents, along with Jasper and Detective Rage came rushing into the living room and outnumbered Malachi.

"Put down the knife, Mr. Townsin," one officer yelled with his gun drawn and aimed at Malachi's face.

He released my arms. I had absolutely no energy to stop them from falling, hard, onto the gaping wound in my abdomen. When I yelled out, Jasper and Rage came running over. Rage grabbed the weapon from Malachi's hand and pulled him off me and to the ground. As he lay on the floor face down, Jasper began kicking him in the ribs. When Malachi turned on his side, Jasper went after his stomach. Rage pushed Jasper away. He came to my aid as Rage knelt down on the back of Malachi's neck.

"Feel grateful I stopped him. I should let him torture and kill your worthless ass."

"He got me again, Jasper. Help me," I said. I was so weak, my voice was barely a whisper and I knew Jasper had to strain to hear me.

"I know baby. Hang in there. Stay with me," he said holding my hand.

A uniformed female officer stood next to me and called on her radio for paramedics. Within minutes, I blacked out.

Twenty-two

When I opened my eyes, it was like de ja vu. Jasper was the first person I saw along with Jillian and Charlotte. I tried to move, but the pain was excruciating.

"What happened this time? What did they do to me?" I asked.

"You received sixteen stitches on the inside. On the outside, the doctor put in about twenty-three stitches. The cuts on your arms and face weren't deep enough to need stitches so they were just cleaned and bandaged," Charlotte said comfortingly.

"What about the babies?" I asked watching the expressions on their faces.

They looked at each other as though they were deciding who would tell me. They mumbled at each other until they all turned back and stared at me, smiling nervously.

"Would some one please tell me what happened to my babies," I said.

"Sweetie, you lost too much blood. The paramedics had a fetal heart monitor on you in the ambulance. By the time you had arrived here, it was too late. They were already gone. Malachi had pierced the amniotic sack when he cut you open. With the babies being so small there was nothing the doctors could do to save them. They performed a D and C. The doctor said you would be bleeding for quite a while as your body flushes out anything left behind. If you need anything I am here for you." Jasper laid it all out for me.

"If I lost so much blood and that is how I lost the babies in the first place, how is it possible for me to lose any more blood to get rid of the babies?"

"You had a blood transfusion. They put most of the blood you lost back," Jillian told me.

I absorbed the information and felt at peace with the decision. Now jasper and I could make our own babies. I inhaled and exhaled deeply. I didn't want to have any connection with the babies anyway. "How long am I going to be here this time?"

Astonished, Charlotte answered, "At least a week."

"Can I be alone for a while? I want to get some sleep."

They left me with my thoughts. I started to cry. I hadn't realized how hard this actually was. I settled in for an extended stay and decided to wait out the duration.

* * *

It was two weeks before I was actually released. Doctor Morgan said my stitches were healing nicely and I was moving around normally, so I could go. After about a month of normal life Charlotte and Jillian decided they wanted to take me on a girls outing vacation.

A couple of days before we left, I went to the police station and Rage allowed me to see the video of the interrogation with Malachi. Charlotte and Jillian, I knew, had been waiting for the moment they could essentially interrogate me about what I had seen and heard.

Jasper was glad to see me go – only because he wanted me to have fun after everything I had been through. He had suggested a road trip so the three of us could talk.

"We will be back in two weeks. We got a fourteen-day relaxation package. We should be back just in time for Malachi's trial. I'm not missing that." I kissed him goodbye after he helped put my luggage into the back of Jillian's SUV.

"Be careful," he warned as we drove down the street.

"So what happened during the interrogation?" Charlotte inquired.

"Rage had asked about his childhood. He wanted to know about the day his parents died."

"Did he say he killed them?"

"No, he said he found them that way. He said he came home from school at the same time he always had. When he stepped over the threshold, he noticed something was different. His mother wasn't standing in the kitchen cooking dinner like she always was. His after school snack wasn't laid out on the dining room table like it always was.

"When he called out for his mother, he said all he heard was silence. He dropped his backpack to the floor at the bottom of the stairs and slowly stepped up making sure both his feet touched each step. At the top of the stairs, he called for his mother again with the same response, silence." I paused for a moment to take a deep breath. "Rage said he spoke in an even tone as though he were telling a story."

"Poor kid comes home from school just to find his parents dead. That must have been traumatizing," Jillian sympathized.

"Now Jilly, this kid is the same psychopath who kidnapped Kenzie and disabled her for life. You do understand that don't you?" Charlotte said.

"Yes, Charlotte, thank you. I just think it is awful for any child to be exposed to something that horrifying." Jillian just shrugged her shoulders then drove staring out the windshield.

"That's enough you two. I haven't even gotten to the parents room yet and you are already judging whether he should be felt sorry for or persecuted for what he did with his life. May I continue without further debate?" I scolded.

Charlotte rolled her eyes and nodded. I noticed there was something strange about the way Jillian was sitting. She normally always had perfect posture, but at this point in time, she was hunched over leaning her head on her hand as she drove. I reached up to the driver's seat and touched her shoulder. She shrugged me away, sat up with her back straight as she always did and peered out the window.

"Are you going to finish telling the story or what?" Jillian spoke harshly, but I knew she didn't mean it.

"Anyway, he said when he had opened his parent's bedroom door, what he had seen was the last thing he had expected. Blood and a lot of it, everywhere. He didn't know how long they had been that way but the blood had already begun to change color. He said it was more like a burgundy rather than red." I continued.

"A little too detailed, don't you think?" Charlotte asked.

"Whatever. I didn't see what it looked like and he was just a kid. This could be something that haunts him and for all we know for him to know what color the blood was at the time that he saw it might be significant for him. If you are done interrupting me now, I can tell you what he saw. I may not have had any photos, but I sure was able to paint a pretty clear picture of it in my mind and it wasn't nice to see."

I took another deep breath, in through my nose, out through my mouth. I looked over at Jillian who was still glaring out the windshield. I knew she was upset and embarrassed about the way Charlotte had treated her. I just never understood why Jillian ever let Charlotte talk to her the way she does. Since the three of us grew up as orphans, that must be what gives us the bond we share.

"He said there was blood on the walls, on the bed, on the floor and on his father. He said at the time it hadn't dawned on him that his father was home from work early.

He wasn't sure what he should do. The crimson liquid had stained the walls as it had rolled down and pooled on the floor. He opened his mouth to yell for help, but changed his mind realizing he was now an orphan and didn't want to be placed into the system.

"His father was sprawled across the bed. A .22 Magnum grasped in his right hand, finger still on the trigger. A self-inflicted gunshot wound to his temple oozed blood and brain matter. He said the liquid was so thick it seemed as though all his blood was escaping from that one hole in his head. His mother's lifeless body was stuffed into a Rubbermaid plastic storage box; her left leg had been removed." I shuttered remembering the feeling of being crammed inside.

"I thought Jasper had said the guy put a shotgun in his mouth and blew out the back of his head?" Charlotte asked.

"I don't know. Maybe the media wanted to make it sound better by saying it was a shotgun rather than a handgun." I replied, shrugging.

"Or maybe Malachi is lying. Maybe he is the liar and not the media. I mean, he is a psychopath. He could be making up the whole story. He could be the real killer. Maybe he shot his dad with the .22 Mag but left him to look like it was a suicide by putting the shotgun in his hand. That could be possible," Jillian analyzed. I was glad she was speaking again.

"That sounds plausible," Charlotte replied.

"Anyway, Rage told me there was a note his father left for him. He said it would be read at the trial so he was going to spare me from hearing it twice." I took another deep breath as Jillian pulled into the parking lot of a beautiful hotel.

I was glad I could stop telling the story and enjoy the scenery. The building was mostly windows wonderfully decorated with exquisite curtains. There were large sliding glass doors that opened to a fifteen by fifteen balcony from each room.

She parked and a bellhop met us with a baggage cart that appeared to be dipped in gold. He helped us unload our luggage from the SUV and loaded it on the cart.

"My name is George Scully. I am going to be your itinerary specialist for the duration of your stay," the bellhop told us after we checked in. "The three of you can relax in the lounge. Your luggage will be waiting for you in your suite."

We headed to a separate room with the words *The Lounge* lit up over the doorway. We sat in three luxurious chaise chairs. They were a light comforting turquoise color. A plush, round floor rug lay beneath the chairs. It was cerulean and grey with yarned in spring flowers.

A beautiful blonde woman with shoulder length hair, wearing a soft pink pantsuit brought over three strawberry sangria's on a silver tray. She placed the tray on the table in the center of the setup then walked away.

We lounged comfortably sipping our drinks. The bellhop returned to us. He handed us each an itinerary, which was printed on lavender paper and set in a keepsake frame.

"How are we doing ladies?" He asked.

"Fantastic, all I need now is a foot rub and I would be in heaven," I commented.

He clapped his hands twice and three Asian ladies wearing baby blue scrubs trotted over, took off our sandals and began rubbing our feet. It was the most amazing, relaxing foot massage I had ever had.

"As you can see by the schedules I have given to you," George began, "I have set up a yoga class for you at seven a.m. Breakfast is served at eight thirty. Your spa appointments are at ten. There you will receive a facial, steam bath and full body massage. At one p.m., you will return to the lounge for lunch. At two thirty, I will meet up with you for a relaxing stroll through the gardens. At four, another yoga session. At five thirty, a hair stylist and make up artist for each of you will meet you in your suite to primp you and help you get ready for dinner. Dinner is served in the restaurant at precisely seven p.m. At nine, a masseur will meet you in your suite for your goodnight massage.

"You are to be in bed at exactly ten p.m. If you have any questions or concerns about your itineraries, please feel free to discuss it with me tomorrow during our stroll. Any failure to show up on time to any scheduled event is a forfeit of relaxation. You will be asked to leave. We have a six-month waiting list and others would be ecstatic to take your place. If there are any emergencies that must be attended to immediately, here are your personalized pagers." George handed each of us a small black remote about three inches long with one red button in the center.

"One press of this button will contact me. I keep the receiver on me at all times. If there is anything at all you may need, day or night, *please* do not hesitate to contact me. It doesn't matter where you are, there is a locator chip, which is activated the second the button is pressed. Are there any questions, hopes, concerns?"

We looked at each other, shook our heads, then relaxed to enjoy the foot rub. The woman rubbing my feet switched from my right foot to my left foot. She looked up at me with a puzzled look on her face.

As I explained to her how I had lost it in a tragic accident, her eyes became sad. She nodded and continued with my right foot. Considering I hadn't told her what kind of accident, I could only imagine what she was thinking.

Twenty-three

The first week was amazing. I hadn't felt that relaxed in over a year. The daily stroll through the garden was immaculate. The smell of the roses, the vision of the well manicured hydrangeas. The grass was the most exquisite emerald green. There were even birds I had never seen before enjoying the scenery.

There were birds that were all black, pitch black as night, with bright crimson rings around their shoulders and an amber stripe on their chest. I had never seen any thing like it.

"George, what kind of bird is that?" I asked.

"That is the Red Winged Black Bird. That one there is the female. We see more of them around then we do the males."

"How can you tell which is male and which is female?"

"The male is always much prettier than the female. The male has a blue almost glow that outlines his wings in which the female does not. In the animal world the male has to present himself to the female in order to be chosen for mating," George explained.

"Kind of like humans," I said laughing.

George laughed too then continued explaining the bird. "The male also has a red ring around its neck and an orangish reddish coloring on its chest."

"That is such a beautiful bird. There isn't anything like it near my house. Every once in a while I'll catch a glimpse of a cardinal in a tree in the back yard but never anything as beautiful as that." It was amazing to watch the birds fly around and interact with each other.

The flowers were blooming and the scent, divine. It was an extraordinarily relaxing walk.

* * *

On day eight, during my goodnight massage, my cell phone rang. The selected tone told me it was Jasper. I excused myself to answer it.

"Hello sweetheart. How has your week been without me?" I asked him.

"I don't mean to ruin your fun, but Detective Rage just called. Malachi managed to escape from custody and another woman has come up missing," Jasper informed.

"What do you mean escaped? I thought he was in a maximum security prison?"

"Well, he was on his way to the maximum security prison when he escaped. It was during transport. Apparently, the bus got a flat on the way out there. The driver stopped to fix it. The guard got off the bus to help and somewhere in the twenty minutes it took to change the tire, he escaped."

"I'm on my way." I hung up the phone and told the masseur I would not be able to finish.

All the relaxed muscles in my back tensed up again. My tranquil state of mind was again frazzled. I began to get dressed. I grabbed the paging device George had given me on the first day and pressed the lone red button. While I waited for him, I packed my suitcase and informed Charlotte and Jillian of the situation.

"We are coming with you," Charlotte said and pulled on her pants.

"No, no. That's not necessary. Ya'll stay here and enjoy the rest of the six days. I'll just fly home," I told them.

"Don't be silly. We're coming with you." Jillian pressed the button on her paging device and Charlotte followed suit.

George finally came to the door of the suite. By then I had realized there was no way I could persuade the two of them in staying.

"We have to leave immediately," I explained. "'The Butcher' has escaped and we have to return to aid the police in his recapture."

The bellhop seemed completely understanding. He helped us to the car with the bags.

Once the luggage was loaded, he handed us VIP passes. "This ensures you a spot on the VIP list. Whenever you can finish your relaxation retreat the VIP list will ensure you a position without being placed on the waiting list.

"It is also a list that is binding for life. No matter how many times you want to come, there will *never* be a wait for relaxation. I thoroughly enjoyed being your liaison for the week. Please request me the next time you are here." He hugged us and told us what a pleasure it was to serve us.

I almost thought at one point I could see a tear glistening in the corner of his eye. The whole drive home was spent discussing how fantastic the last eight days had been.

Twenty-four

"When we searched Malachi's home we had un-covered a couple of notes with her signature," Detective Rage said. He had asked Jasper and I to join him to interview a neighbor who lived across the street from Corbin and Dina Townsin during the murder-suicide.

"Do you think she knew he was 'The Butcher'?" I asked.

"Here," Rage handed me a piece of paper.

I unfolded it and read it quietly to myself.

Dear Malachi,

I'm worried about you. You haven't been returning my phone calls or writing back as often as before. I've been thinking about coming for a visit. I so miss our visits. I enjoyed the way we used to sit and chat over coffee (even if it was at a diner instead of your home).

Please, Malachi, don't shut me out. I'm the only connection you have to your mother; as well, you are mine to her. I still miss her dearly. I just wish her death wasn't being splattered all over the news. They are comparing a murder that happened in Dallas to what happened to your mother. Every time another girl dies, the police come over to snoop around my house. You have to turn yourself in. What you are doing is wrong.

Malachi, I'm begging you. Please call or write soon.

Love always,

Brooke Kendall

"It sounds to me that she knew exactly what he was doing. She knew he was killing these women and I bet she never told anyone," I said as I handed the letter back to Rage.

"That's what I thought too. I figured you could help asking her why. I know you want to know why he did this to you. Maybe she knows why he is psycho," Rage said.

"I can see why he left town. Every one probably thought he was a killer and he fled as far as his allowance would take him. He is only a six hour drive back home, but maybe he stayed in the state in order to visit his parent's grave sites. You know, birthdays, holidays. Stupid sappy shit," Jasper contributed to the conversation.

"Of course, honey. You know how sentimental murderers can be," I told him, sarcastically.

"You never know. Maybe he has a softer side," Rage laughed.

Being in a car with a cop-on-a-mission driving, it was great to be able to make a six hour drive into four. As we pulled into the driveway of Brooke Kendall's house, I noticed the fresh new paint job to the exterior gave her home a new look. I would have never thought her house was built in the sixties.

Rage folded up the letter and placed it into the breast pocket of his dress shirt. The three of us approached the front door and Rage rang the doorbell. Her well-manicured lawn was the perfect view while waiting.

When the door opened, a lovely brunette lady, who had to be well into her fifties, but didn't look a day over thirty-eight, stood wearing a perfectly pressed blouse. Her skirt, which fell just below her knees, was the sight of perfection as well. Not a hair was out of place, nor a run in her stockings.

"Mrs. Kendall, my name is Detective Rage. This is Jasper Tully and Mackenzie Leigh. May we come in? I would like to ask you a few questions about Malachi Townsin."

"Of course, please come in. Come in," she stepped aside and closed the door behind us. "Would anyone like any thing to drink? I have water, coffee, iced tea."

We stood in the foyer looking at each other. The house was exquisite.

"I would love some iced tea, thank you." I was the first to speak.

"That sounds wonderful. I would also love some iced tea," Jasper agreed.

Rage also requested iced tea. We were so overwhelmed by the beauty of her home.

"Please come in. Make yourselves at home," she said motioning us to the living room.

"Everything is so clean. There doesn't look like there is a speck of dirt or dust anywhere," I whispered to Jasper as we headed to the seating area.

Her house was just as immaculate as her appearance. The navy blue sofa, as far as I could tell, was vacuumed everyday. Not one little spot, stain or crumb occupied any part of it. Her grayish-white carpet appeared brand new.

"So Detective, what can I do for you?" Brooke asked brandishing a freshly polished silver tray with four glasses of iced tea, four small plates and a pie that smelled fresh out of the oven.

"How well did you know the Townsins?" Rage began the interview.

"Dina came over everyday as did three other housewives."

"Could you explain to me a normal week for the five of you?"

"Around ten a.m., after all our housework was done, the girls would come over."

"Can you tell me the names and some information about the other three ladies?" Rage asked.

"There's Wendy Hollow, she's the youngest of us all and has the most children. She's had seven kids in eighteen years. Each is three years apart and amazingly enough, well behaved.

"Then there's Robin Sort. She's a freelance copywriter with two children. Poor things a widow. Her husband, Jim, was a Marine. He was deployed to Iraq a few years back. She was on her way over here one morning. It was her turn to bring the mid-morning snack. The military officers told her, Jim's military barracks had been attacked in the middle of the night. Twenty Marines were killed.

"She dropped an entire basket of freshly baked mini quiches right to the ground. It took a week and a half to get her out of bed. Her house was always clean thanks to me as well as her children being taken care of.

"Next is Jocelyn Martin. She doesn't do anything. Never had any children, but has been married numerous times. She lives off alimony and settlement money from all her husbands. She knows how to invest her money wisely and always seems to choose the men who cheat. They are always rich, but always have an over active sexual appetite. If you ask me I think she drives them to cheat on her just so she can collect their money."

I guessed that out of the five women, Brooke was the gossip. She seemed to know everything about everyone.

"How much did you know about Dina's son?"

"I knew that he was twelve at the time of the tragedy. He was always quiet and kept to himself. Although, every time I went over to the house he was always polite and said hello."

"Do *you* have any children, Mrs. Kendall?" Jasper asked.

"No, Mr. Tully, I don't. I have always been the designated neighborhood babysitter. I have had the chance to get to know and see all of the children grow up on this block. In a sense I have over fifteen children." She sounded a little insulted that he would have even thought about asking about her personal life.

Rage decided to take over the interview again. "Mrs. Kendall, the initial investigation records show you were interviewed about the Townsin murder-suicide. If you could fill in anything that was left out and possibly help locate Malachi, it would be greatly appreciated."

Brooke took a deep breath, closed her eyes as though she were thinking back. She reopened her eyes and began. "The detective that questioned me, I believe his name was Gary, I didn't know whether that was his first name or his last, he began by asking what time it was when I stopped by the crime scene. I told him it was around three." Her eyes sort of glazed over as though she were having a flash back as she recalled the interview on that tragic day.

'That was when the boy answered the door?'

"Detective Gary asked, and I nodded in agreement," Brooke explained.

'Was there anything unusual about his behavior?'

'Yes, he seemed very nervous, like he was in a hurry and trying to get rid of me.'

'Do you think that was the result of finding his parents dead or an admission of guilt for killing them?'

'He didn't kill his parents, detective. With as much blood that I saw, he would have had some on him as well. Oh, there was so much blood.' Tears welled up in her eyes as she reminisced.

'What time did he usually get home from school?'

'Around two forty-five. There was no way he could have killed his parents and cleaned up in fifteen minutes.'

'Do you think it is possible he left school early to come home to murder his parents?'

'No, I saw him get off the bus. And he didn't come home, murder his parents then go back to school. Dina left my house around one thirty because Corbin came home early.'

'Were they arguing? Did you hear any gun shots?'

'I left my house around two to run to the grocery store to pick up a few things for dinner. If they were arguing they were doing it quietly.'

'What time was it when you discovered the bodies?'

'I know it was about five. I came over to find out if everything was okay.'

'Was the boy still here?'

'No, but the back gate was open and the ATV was missing from the shed.'

'So you think the boy fled the crime scene? Seems suspicious don't you think?'

"Detective Gary tapped his pen on his notebook and raised his eyebrows at me."

'Malachi is a good boy. He gets straight A's and always does as he is told. Just because he is a twelve year old boy does not make him a hooligan.'

'Some teenagers who appear well behaved on the outside sometimes snap one day and resent their parents. Most of them just rebel, but there are the select few who go as far as murder. Remember the Menendez brothers? This could be the beginning of a very dangerous person. We are having the gun tested for prints.'

Brooke shook her head as though she were coming back to reality. "I remember being so mad I stepped up to him, standing on my tip-toes attempting to get face to face with him, but my five foot two inch frame compared to his six foot three inches, I was face to chin. He continued to accuse that poor boy, so I walked away from him. The girls came over and we sat around mourning the death of our friend."

"We have reason to believe you have kept in touch with Malachi and knew what he was doing," Rage blurted.

"What makes you think that? I haven't seen or spoken to the boy since that night," Brooke said with a guilty look on her face.

We could all tell she was lying. Rage pulled out the letter and tossed it in front of her on the coffee table. She picked it up and skimmed her eyes over the words. I watched her face change from guilt to sadness.

"Okay, I admit, we had kept in touch for quite a few years. We exchanged letters and I called him a few times. Is it a crime to keep in contact with someone?" Brooke's eyes welled up with tears, again.

"Actually, it is a crime not to report a known criminal. It seems as though you knew it was him all along. If you knew he was killing people why didn't you go to the police and report him?" Rage asked.

"I wasn't absolutely sure if it was really him. He never actually came out and told me."

"Was there ever a time when you discussed the murders or the victims with him?"

"There was this one telephone conversation we had. I had just seen a news report about another girl who had been murdered. As a matter of fact I think it was right before the report about you Mackenzie." Brooke made eye contact with me.

"You mean to tell me that if you had just reported him to the police you could have saved me from this whole traumatic experience?" I stood over her as the anger boiled to the surface and began to overflow.

Jasper stood and wrapped his arms around my waist. "Sit down sweetie. Let's just listen to what she has to say."

I sat back down on the sofa next to Jasper. I nodded and breathed through my nose to bury the monster building inside.

"Mrs. Kendall, can you recall that phone conversation for us?" Rage asked.

Brooke nodded. Her eyes glazed over again as she slipped back into a flashback.

"I was crying when I called him. There was a news story about Dina again and I remembered how much I missed her. I called Malachi to hear a familiar voice of someone I had lost. He had even initially asked if I had been crying.

'Only because of something I saw on the news,' I had told Malachi.

'What did you see?' He asked me."

'Another girl was found with her leg cut off like your mother.'

'Don't worry about that. It's just a news story. You know how the media can embellish stories and make them sound worse than they really are.'

"Malachi just seemed to be blowing off the whole situation."

'It's not just this one girl. There have been more. These women died the same way your mother did. Malachi, what's going on down there?'

Brooke was crying, but her face showed no true emotion. The look in her eyes was distant.

'What apparently is going on around here is there is a killer on the loose. Luckily he is only killing women so I guess I don't have anything to worry about it.'

"Malachi chuckled. I couldn't tell if he was laughing to make me feel better, or if he was seriously deranged and he thought his actions were funny."

'The situation is not funny. How can you laugh this off?'

'Look, what happened to my parents was a nightmare. The copycat killer is keeping their memory alive and I applaud him.'

'How can you say that? Malachi, the person recreating your mother's horrible murder is sick. This person needs help.'

"I was treading the water of a possibly unstable person and I knew it. I was trying to get him to admit that he had committed those murders."

'Look Brooke, I don't know what you think you are trying to do, but whatever it is you better watch what you say.'

"Malachi was so angry I could tell he was talking through clenched teeth."

'Alright, I'm sorry. How about I change the subject? Are you seeing anyone these days?'

"I was trembling with fear and trying not to let it be heard in my voice. I didn't want him to think he frightened me. I figured that would give him too much power over me. I knew he was capable of killing me whenever he wanted."

'Actually there is someone. Her name is Mackenzie Leigh. She has chocolate brown hair, the most beautiful green eyes and an hourglass figure. She has one of the best smiles I have ever seen. When she talks it almost sounds as though she is singing.'

'She sounds wonderful. I just wish you would move back to Austin. You could stay with me and I could lead you back on the right path.'

'You know I can't do that Brooke. People there know who I am. They know what I've done and they would turn me in, in a heartbeat. Now please stop pressing the matter.'

Brooke blinked her eyes quickly as she came back to the present. Tears streaming down her cheeks. "I'm so sorry, Mackenzie. Maybe I could have saved you if I had only told someone what I suspected. When he mentioned you, he gave so much detail, I thought you were someone he was dating not someone he was stalking."

Rage stood up, motioned for Brooke to stand, handcuffed her. "Brooke Kendall, you are under arrest. You have the right to remain silent..." He recited the Miranda rights to her.

We all knew why she was being arrested. Hopefully, a judge would have mercy on her. She seemed genuinely sorry for not telling.

Twenty-five

When we returned to the police station, the officer at the front desk told Rage there were three women waiting for him in interrogation room two. He left Brooke in interrogation room one with Jasper and me, then went to meet with the other ladies.

She was still cuffed and the fire that still burned inside me was aching to get out. I wanted to lunge at her. I wanted to bury my fist into her face. Just thinking that she could have saved other women and me, I couldn't believe she kept what she knew about him to herself. I may have forgiven her, but I was still angry.

"I'm really sorry Mackenzie. If I had any idea at all that if I just told someone I thought it was him and that it would have saved a lot of women their lives, I would have told. I just didn't think it would make a difference," Brooke admitted, tears streaming down her face, smearing her mascara.

"Well, you got one thing right. You didn't think," I retorted.

"I think it would be best if you didn't speak," Jasper told Brooke.

She looked down at the table. Jasper sat across from her and I paced the room. Finally, Rage returned and motioned for Jasper and I to join him in the hallway.

"The three ladies in the next room are the friends Brooke had mentioned at her home. They have some pretty interesting things to say about the Townsin boy. You wouldn't believe how many times they went to the police about Malachi. Because they only had suspicion and no real reason why he was the killer, the police wouldn't do anything. The girls tried to get Brooke to come with them and show the police the letters, but she refused, claiming he was a good boy and there was no way he could have committed any of the murders." Rage spoke quietly so Brooke couldn't hear our conversation through the door.

I thought about the load of bullshit she had just tried to feed me and explained to Rage what she had said about five minutes before he had opened the door.

He snorted and gave me a face that proved he didn't believe her story either. "The letter we have says otherwise. You should really go talk to her friends. They could possibly shed some light on her reasoning."

He swung his arm in a motion for Jasper and me to follow him into interrogation room two.

"Mackenzie Leigh, Jasper Tully, this is Jocelyn Martin, Robin Sort and Wendy Hollow. Ladies, would you please tell them what you told me." Rage pulled out two chairs for us to sit.

Jocelyn began, "The day Malachi's parents died, once the police were done questioning us, we headed over to Brooke's house and sat around the breakfast table. She brought out a platter full of cookies and a carafe of coffee. Brooke was the only one of us that wanted to find him."

"We all told her to let the police find him. I said I didn't even think the police would look for him unless they found any evidence that pointed toward him as the killer. I figured if they didn't find anything to accuse a twelve-year-old boy of a double murder they would just write it off as a murder-suicide and pretend Corbin and Dina never had any children. Case closed." Wendy continued the conversation.

"Brooke went on telling us we should look for him. She said there was no telling what kind of psychological damage could have been done to him from the exposure of the scene he had witnessed. We all assumed it had something to do with her never having children and wanting to raise a troubled child." Robin sounded disturbed.

"If we had known it was because she had suspected he was the killer we would have talked her into going to the police that day to tell them her suspicions." Jocelyn concluded.

"She claims she is sure he didn't kill his parents. Was there ever an indication where she may have slipped or said anything incriminating?" Jasper inquired.

"Did she ever tell any of you *she* suspected Malachi had killed his parents?" I asked.

"Not ever that he had killed his parents, but there was this one time when we were watching a news story about one of the victims and she stopped herself from revealing any incriminating evidence. The three of us thought she knew more than what she was leading us to believe."

"What did she say?"

"The news anchor mentioned the name of the victim and Brooke gasped. When I asked if anything was wrong she played it off and said she used to know someone by that name. When I pressed for more information she said she must have been mistaken and she just said the name sounded familiar." Jocelyn was now very animated with her gestures as she spoke.

"From that day on, we knew she had been talking to him, even though she wouldn't admit it," Wendy said.

"She had told me at one time when we were alone that she felt all the killings could have been avoided if only she had raised him. When I asked her what she meant by that, she blew it off as though I heard her incorrectly. I knew what I heard and knew what it meant, but hoped one day she would confide in her friends and tell us what she knew," Robin said reluctantly.

"You never told us about that," Wendy and Jocelyn said simultaneously with a hurt look on each of their faces.

Robin looked down at the table as though she were ashamed. The anger I felt for Brooke was now shared with her friends. I had nothing left to say to them. I turned and stormed out of the room.

All the stress I had been through over the past six months had caught up with me. The second I stepped out the front doors of the police station and the heat hit my face I began to hyperventilate. My breathing quickened, my chest became tight, my hands, face and back felt like millions of pins were trapped inside my body and they were poking to get out. I was having a panic attack. I dropped to the ground. My prosthetic leg was not helping at that point. All the muscles in my body had tightened and I had no control over the one part of my body that needed the most concentration and control of all.

With very little oxygen getting to my brain, my sensory receptors were failing. Black spots circled in silver appeared in my line of sight; my hearing was altered as though earplugs had been installed. I blacked out and fell into a state of unconsciousness.

Twenty-six

When I opened my eyes and looked around I felt disoriented, but relieved I wasn't in the hospital. I sat up slowly. I was on a tattered old sofa that reeked of stale cigarette smoke. The room was dark other than strips of light sneaking in through the cracks of the blinds. There was a desk in the room, but no one sitting behind it.

I walked over and opened the door. Jasper, Charlotte and Jillian sat on a wooden bench just outside the room.

"Are you okay?" Charlotte asked as she approached me with a hug.

"I'm fine. How long have I been out? Are the police on a man hunt?"

"They have called in for more FBI agents. Several different agencies have sent help to find Malachi," Jasper informed me.

"What good are they going to do us now? We already know who we are looking for." I stormed off to find Detective Rage.

I spotted him in a room surrounded by windows. Rage was sitting at a conference table surrounded by five other federal agents. They were looking over photos of the victims. I thrust the door open feeling as though they were wasting time.

"How is this helping? How is sitting around a table the same as catching and arresting Malachi?" I yelled.

"Calm down Mackenzie. These agents are here to help us figure out where he would go," Rage explained.

"Mrs. Leigh, I'm agent Daria. We have concluded Mr. Townsin would be less likely to return to his home with his latest victim. The house is still closed off. Caution tape…"

"Wait a minute, latest victim?" I interrupted. "He's taken someone else?"

"Earlier this morning a nine-one-one call was received by a woman claiming her twenty six year old daughter never came home last night. The operator asked for a description of her daughter. The operator passed it on to the police and now we are on alert to help find Malachi and the girl because her description matches the other victims," Rage said.

"Why would they show up to help find an escapee? Isn't that the job of the local police?" I asked, still peeved.

"That's true; the sheriff this time had asked to enlist our help to figure out where the suspect would go considering his comfort zone has been compromised." Agent Daria stood and stepped toward me.

Her classic grey pantsuit was set off by a deep purple blouse. The two-color clash almost made her look like a bruise. Her footwear suggested she dressed in the dark. She had slipped her petit feet into a pair of silver pumps.

"There is a woman in one of the interrogation rooms…" My voice trailed off as I watched Rage shake his head.

"She has been released, Mackenzie," Rage said.

"WHAT!" I yelled. "I can't believe you let her go."

"While you were resting, two agents went in and spoke with Brooke. She was cleared to go." Rage returned to his seat at the head of the conference table.

"Fine, ya'll can sit here and pretend to work while my friends and I go catch a killer." I turned and walked out the door.

Agent Daria followed. I motioned for Jasper, Charlotte and Jillian to follow me. I left the police station with the four of them in tow. As soon as we were about ten feet from the station, I turned around to address everyone.

"If you would like to help Agent Daria, please feel free to jump in at anytime with any advice you may have. Otherwise you can just turn around and go back to the group of agents sitting around doing nothing."

She shook her head. "Please proceed."

"Good, now that we have the help of a federal agent this could be a lot easier. First, we start in the obvious places just to rule them out. We can start at his house. That is the most obvious. After that, we can go to the diner. Then, we will look outside the box." I began and drew a box with my fingers in the air.

"I wanna help," a female voice said from behind me.

I turned to see a woman who appeared to be in her early thirties. She stood about five feet four inches tall. She was wearing denim Capri's with a black t-shirt, which had a very large pink hibiscus flower printed on the front. Her brown sandals completed her ensemble. Her blonde hair was showing brunette roots.

"Who are you?" I asked.

"My name is Ansley Kirkland. I was a victim of 'The Butcher'." Everyone's jaws dropped open and she continued. "I was found in the woods approximately one hundred fifty miles from the nearest hospital. There is a diner not far from here. We can sit and have coffee and I will tell you my story."

"How about we go back into the police station and we can talk to the lead detective on this case," Agent Daria said, trying to usher us back.

"I came here to talk to the other survivor and her family, not the police. I do not want my story to be announced to the public so I can be back on his radar. I want to keep quiet about my survival," Ansley said, standing face to face with Daria.

"This is a police matter. The case is still under investigation. The lead detective on this case has all right to know your story."

"Then I hope you know how to take good notes."

We each agreed and the five of us followed Ansley down the street. As we walked, I noticed both her legs looked identical. She walked without a limp, unlike me. If she was a victim of 'The Butcher', how did she get away with both legs? I was still having trouble getting used to my prosthetic. It rubbed my thigh raw. I constantly had muscle cramps.

I envied this woman. If she did have a prosthetic, she was probably determined to walk normal again as was I. I was just still wallowing in self-pity inside.

We sauntered inside and sat down at a large booth in the far corner. Agent Daria opened the portfolio she had been carrying and started taking notes. After the waitress brought us our coffee, Ansley reached down and removed her prosthetic left leg. I almost doubted her credibility up until then. I couldn't believe how real it looked.

"It was about four years ago. He took me from my home. He was already in the apartment when I arrived. He forced me to change into an outfit I would never wear," Ansley began.

"He did the same to me," I put in.

"Once I was dressed I thought he would leave, but before I knew it he was behind me. He smothered my nose and mouth with a cloth," she continued, as though I hadn't spoken. Her eyes welled up with tears and I felt sympathy for her.

"He did the same to me, Ansley. I went through it too."
I touched her shoulder and she leaned over and hugged me.

She brushed away her tears as she pulled away and continued. "When I regained consciousness I was tied to a chair. It was like a dentist's chair. There was a light attached overhead and a metal tray to the left of me with hand tools lying straight and organized on top. I was a psychologist and had a master's degree in behavior. I noticed this as a classic sign of obsessive-compulsive disorder. After a while, I didn't know how much time had passed, he returned. I was sexually assaulted. He touched and raped me." The tears returned to her eyes and she had to stop for a moment.

"It's over now, Mrs. Kirkland. He can't hurt you any more," Agent Daria spoke.

"You're not helping any," I said. "He did the same to me. Although, when he raped me, I was tied to the bed and it resulted in a pregnancy. When I was four and a half months along I gave myself up to him and he tried to cut out the babies. By the time Jasper and Detective Rage got to me, I had lost so much blood and my twins. I had already accepted them as my own even though they were a result of a tragedy." As I watched her cry, I realized she wasn't as strong emotionally as she was physically.

"My son is now three," Ansley revealed. "After he violated me, he placed a clamp in my mouth, reclined the chair back and proceeded to remove my teeth. He started with the molars and moved his way to the incisors. I could feel the blood pouring from my mouth. All he used was a pair of pliers. Once I was feeling weak and woozy from the blood loss he untied each hand, one at a time and broke my thumbs. Then, he untied my feet and carried me to a bed. I had no fight left in me.

"As he bound me to the bed, I passed out. I was only out for a few moments. I was awakened when he threw cold water on my face. It helped rinse the metallic taste of the blood out of my mouth. He snapped a few photos of me. He stepped up to the left side of the bed, picked up a metal baseball bat and swung it twice striking my knee. I could feel the bones shattering under the pressure of the blows. He placed the bat meticulously against the wall in line with a wood chopping hatchet and a machete. He then admired himself in front of a full-length mirror that hung on the wall. After retrieving the machete, he again stood to the left of me and hacked off my leg. He took a few more pictures, then left the room.

"I again passed out. When I woke up the final time, I was inside a cabin with a woman who was cleaning and bandaging my wounds. I have been hiding out and living there with her ever since." Ansley took a deep breath and replaced her prosthetic leg.

"Who was the woman who found you?" I asked.

"Her name is Gabrielle Whitton. She found me in the woods behind her house. She was out walking her dogs. The golden retriever found me in a Rubbermaid storage box. She loaded the box with me inside onto a wheelbarrow and took me back to her house. She had an extensive first aid kit with a stethoscope and realized I was still alive. She cauterized my wounds and kept me alive for three days until I regained consciousness. She told me to stay as long as I liked."

"How did you get a leg that looks so real?"

"I was lucky when I found out she came from a large family of doctors. Her younger brother is a prosthetic specialist. It only took a few months for him to produce a leg and foot that matched identically. He could do something for you so it doesn't look so plastic."

"Your teeth look amazing. I couldn't even tell they weren't real," I said, hoping to take the conversation off the fact that I have a plastic leg.

"Gabrielle's older brother is a dentist."

"She sounds like an amazing woman," Jillian commented.

"She really is. She helped me though the pregnancy as well as delivering the baby. She has allowed me to hide out there for the past four years. She treats me like a member of her family. She is a veterinarian, but still knew how to talk me through the birthing process."

I only wore capris pants and close toed sandals on our vacation, other than that I had been wearing jeans and tennis shoes in order to hide my plastic leg. I was amazed to see her wearing flip-flops. I was actually envious of this girl.

"What are you expecting to accomplish by admitting all of this? Can we speak to this woman to corroborate your story?" Agent Daria sounded skeptical.

"I figured I could help. I am more than willing to introduce you to Gabrielle Whitton." If looks could kill, Agent Daria would have dropped dead right there on the floor from the offended look on Ansley's face. "Let me call her and let her know we are coming so she isn't surprised when I show up with a group."

We left the diner and headed out to our vehicles. Agent Daria and Ansley climbed onto a black four-door sedan - probably government issued - Jasper, Jillian, Charlotte and I all piled into Jillian's SUV. We followed the car for forty-five minutes deep into the wood.

Twenty-seven

Gabrielle Whitton's house was a two-bedroom log cabin. It looked as though it were built forty years ago. The wood was stacked up horizontally and nailed together in all the right places. From the outside, it looked like it only had one floor, but when we stepped through the front door into the cozy living room, there was a staircase. At the top of the stairs was the only full bathroom in the house. There was a half bathroom behind the stairs between the only two bedrooms in the house.

The open floor plan allowed us to see the kitchen and what I assumed was a dining/storage room. The table was clear, but against each wall was stacked floor to ceiling with boxes.

"Have a seat, please. Make yourselves at home," Gabrielle said.

The inside of the house did not mirror the outside. The historical appearance was preserved in the shell, even though the interior had been refurbished with intricately designed plush carpet, soft beige painted walls and an accommodating tan microfiber sectional sofa.

"The décor is exquisite Ms. Whitton," I told her as I smoothed my hand along the arm of the sofa.

"Please call me Gabrielle. That actually has a pull out sofa bed in it. I know it is a little cramped in here but it fits pretty well when it is pulled out," she informed me.

The kitchen had smooth marble tile flooring that matched the granite countertop. Her stainless steel appliances really tied the whole room together; as did the oak cabinets being a perfect match to the oak dining table.

She brought out tea and sesame crackers as she joined us in the living room. "As you can tell, due to the space issue, I don't entertain much. Ansley, why don't you grab a few chairs from the dining room so our guests don't have to sit on top of each other," Gabrielle said.

Ansley obeyed. The sofa was actually the perfect size for the five us. There was even enough room for a couple more if we squished together.

"So Ansley tells me ya'll want to talk to me and ask a few questions. Is that right agent?" She put all her focus on Agent Daria.

"Yes ma'am. When was the first time you came into contact with Mrs. Kirkland and what was her condition?" Daria began.

"It had to have been about four years ago if Matthew is about three now. She was close to death. Her heartbeat was faint and irregular. There was blood all over her body and at first I couldn't tell where it was coming from. I was glad I was able to get her inside. I grabbed my first aid kit, cleaned her up and bandaged her wounds.

"I'm a veterinarian and have many times saved wounded dogs close to death after being hit by a car. I didn't know if I could save a human, but I had to do something. She would have died if I had waited for the paramedics. I couldn't have lived with myself if I knew I could have done something."

"Once you fixed her up and knew she was going to survive, why didn't you call for the paramedics then?" Daria grilled.

"Well I had recognized her wounds as a trademark of 'The Butcher'. I figured once she arrived at the hospital the media would hear about a survivor of 'The Butcher' and he would know he didn't kill her and try to come after her again to finish her off. I don't know what I would do if I knew I was the one responsible for putting her back in danger." A single tear escaped from Gabrielle's left tear duct and slowly ran down her cheek.

Ansley stood and walked over to her caretaker placing her hands on Gabrielle's shoulders. Gabrielle reached up with her left hand and placed it on Ansley's right hand.

"I think we have heard enough. Agent Daria, I don't know what you were expecting to find out, but I think we got the whole story," I said as I stood.

"Thank you Mrs. Whitton for your hospitality. Ansley you are a strong woman and I hope you are willing to testify at the trial once we find this sick son of a bitch," Jasper said.

"I want to help Mackenzie find him. I understand you met someone who knew this man personally?" Ansley asked.

"I did. Would you like to go to her house with me? She lives up in Austin," I replied.

"I don't think that would be a good idea, Ansley. I think you should just continue to hide here until we are sure 'The Butcher' is dead," Gabrielle commented.

"Even if he is arrested, convicted and sentenced to death row, it could be decades before the sentence is carried out," Ansley refuted.

"Ansley, I feel that you could be walking right into danger. Please think about it."

Ansley turned to face me. "I would love to go. We can leave in the morning. Would you like to meet Matthew? He is in the backyard playing." She led Jillian, Charlotte and I out to a small fenced in area in the back of the property.

There was a small toe headed boy playing on a play set that looked like a pirate ship. It was setup in the center of the fencing. There were two large dogs standing guard at the entrance. They lay down as soon as Ansley opened the gate. The little boy ran over, jumped up into Ansley's arms and shouted, "Mama!"

"Oh Ansley, he's gorgeous," I said.

Charlotte and Jillian made instant friends with the golden retriever and yellow Labrador. Now I was envious of her and her child. I wondered what my twins would have looked like. I decided at that point as soon as all of this was over, Jasper and I were going to try for a baby.

"Well Ansley, I'm glad that your life has taken a turn for the better even after the horrific ordeal you went through. I hope that someday I will be able to live without having to look over my shoulder and feeling like someone is following me." I gave her a hug.

"I hide here. I am always looking over my shoulder being afraid he is going to come back for me. You are the reason I came out of hiding," she said before releasing from the embrace.

I told her I would pick her up around eight thirty the next morning.

Twenty-eight

That night Jasper and I sat with Charlotte and Jillian on the back patio at Jasper's house. For a long while, no one said anything. It wasn't until Charlotte, who has always hated silence, decided to start the conversation.

"That is so sad, what happened to Ansley. The fact that she kept the baby shows courage and strength."

"Uh, hello. It happened to me too, remember?" I lifted my shirt to expose the scar across my abdomen. "Twice, as a matter of fact."

"I know, but you have people who love and support you. She doesn't. Or at least didn't at the time she was dumped into the woods like someone's garbage. The fact is that Gabrielle took her in and is helping her raise her baby. That makes her a hero." Charlotte inhaled and exhaled deeply as though she idolized Gabrielle.

"You know, we really don't know anything about her family. She never said anything about her mother, father, or whether or not she had any siblings," Jillian pointed out.

"That's true. We don't know anything about her back story. Who exactly is Ansley Kirkland, if that is her real name," Charlotte conceived.

"I know one thing for sure, if she is legit, as soon as this is all over and Ansley feels safe enough to come out of hiding, I think the two of us should start a support group for others who have lost a limb in tragedy. She has really inspired me. Maybe I'll talk to her about it on our way out to

Brook's house tomorrow." This idea made me begin to feel like I had something to look forward to with the rest of my life.

"Maybe you should find out who she is first. Ask her some questions about her background and family," Charlotte told me.

"If everything checks out okay, you and Ansley can do research on what it takes to do something like that. If you have all the information you need to get it started, when we get back from our honeymoon you should be able to jump right in and do that," Jasper lent his support.

"Not only that, but you could also council women who are the victims of rape," Jillian suggested.

"That's a great idea. Thanks ya'll. I'm so glad at least two of you are being supportive." I peered over at Charlotte.

"I'm just saying, you know how crazy people can be. Even people you would never suspect. You just need to be careful," Charlotte warned.

Just then, the doorbell rang. "Who would be coming over at this time of night?" Jasper asked as he rose. He walked through the house to answer the door.

When he returned, he was carrying a box. It looked identical to the others.

"He's doing it again. He is trying to upset me so I will give in to him. Well not any more. No matter what is in that box, I am not going to let it lower my self-esteem or allow myself to feel guilty. I have no reason to feel guilty. Just because I survived does not make it my fault that he continues to kill people." A little bit of guilt passed through my tough exterior and my eyes filled with tears.

Jasper placed the box down on the patio at my feet. I reached down and opened the box. I first pulled out the letter, then the photos and the infamous video. I held everything in my hands not really wanting to see the victim he portrayed as his play toy. The others sat anxiously awaiting the reveal.

I slowly set down the pictures; one at a time on the patio table, carefully spreading them out so each one could be seen completely. These photos seemed more gruesome than the others did. The girl in the photos was unrecognizable. Her face was slashed so many times blood was covering her features. Even her hair was smothered in the crimson liquid.

I read the letter aloud. This one wasn't as nice as the others were.

"Look bitch. I don't know what else I have to do to convince you that it is your time to die. I will not stop until you are six feet underground. I've got you twice now. The third time you won't be so lucky. Just look at the pictures of Carrie Sutton. I will do the same to you. I have chosen my sharpest field dressing knife so I can gut you like a deer." I took a gander at a few of the photos. I tried to count all the gashes on her face, but after twenty five I began feeling sick to my stomach.

I continued reading. *"Once your insides are on the outside there is no one who can save you. Remember this, I will not stop until you are dead.*

"Sincerely your reaper, 'The Butcher'."

I placed the letter down on the table with the other paraphernalia. I didn't know what to say.

Charlotte, of course, was the first to break the silence. "Why did he sign it 'The Butcher' if he knows we know who he is?"

"I don't know. Maybe because it's his trademark. In his own sick and twisted way maybe he thinks he is being funny," I told her. I stood and went into the house.

I decided I was done for the night and went into the bedroom to dress for bed. As I was removing my leg, Jasper came through the door.

"Are you okay honey? Jillian and Charlotte are leaving and they wanted to say good-bye."

"I'll be out in a minute." I grabbed my crutches and followed Jasper out to the foyer.

"Are you sure you don't want us to go with you tomorrow to talk to Brooke?" Jillian asked.

"I'm sure, I'll be fine. Ansley and I can take care of ourselves." I gave Jillian a hug then turned to Charlotte.

"You don't really know Ansley that well and you don't know if she is even really legit."

"Charlotte, what is that supposed to mean? She's not really an amputee or what?" I asked a little offended.

"That's not what I meant. What I meant was how can you be sure she was really a victim of 'The Butcher'? Maybe she is in cahoots with Malachi and she is going to help him get you the third and final time," Charlotte told me as she placed a hand on my shoulder.

"You're talking crazy. She took off her prosthetic leg. Something happened that caused her to lose her leg and I am sure any excuses you would come up with are probably stupid. I don't need you tagging along giving Ansley the third degree. Good-bye, Charlotte." I turned and headed back to the bedroom.

"Good job Charlotte," I heard Jillian say. "I hope she's not mad at me too."

Shortly after I heard the front door close, Jasper came back into the bedroom. I lay down in bed as he did his nightly ritual. Afterward, he joined me laying by my side.

I felt his hand move from my knee to my chest as he stroked my body. His fingers lingered over my breasts as he leaned in to kiss me. His mouth over took mine and our tongues intertwined.

He gently kissed my cheek and slowly his lips traveled down my body. With each soft touch, I moaned. That night Jasper made love to me for the first time.

Twenty-nine

After I picked up Ansley, she began rambling on about how excited she was. I don't know what she was excited about; my mind was rolling around the idea of her and I working together. I wasn't sure how I would ask her. I was afraid she would say no. I didn't know if my self-esteem could handle the rejection.

I did, however, tell her about the package I had received the night before as well as the two previous.

"Oh man, I don't think I could handle that as well as you have. I think I would have committed suicide!" Ansley pronounced emphatically.

"It has been hard. I am just lucky to have the people I do around me. Jasper has been sweet and wonderful. Charlotte and Jillian stick by me no matter what. I probably would have slit my wrists in the tub until the water ran as red as a rose," I replied.

"You are very lucky to have such a supportive family." Ansley looked down at her hands on her lap.

"So, Ansley, how does your family feel about you hiding out in a stranger's house, or do they think you're still missing after four years?" I asked, just jumping right into the subject.

"My parents died in a car accident when I was twelve. I never had any siblings as were my parents only children. I never knew my grandparents an either side and my parents never had a will, so even child services didn't know where to place me.

"I bounced around from foster home to foster home until I was eighteen and moved out on my own. I kept to myself, never made any friends and made sure not to get too close to anyone so I could just be that person whose parents died and that was it."

I reached over and placed my hand on her shoulder. "Don't worry, Ansley. We are connected from a tragedy and will always be. I hope you feel you can count on me as well as Jasper, Charlotte and Jillian just as you could family."

Ansley looked up at me and smiled. "Thank you."

I turned down the street Brooke's house was located and parked the car out front by the curb. The two of us exited the vehicle and walked up to the front door. I rang the doorbell and we waited. After about a minute, I pressed the button again which chimed the bell a second time. After another minute, I reached up to knock on the door.

Before my knuckles came into contact with the pinewood, I noticed it was open a smidge. I pushed it open with my fingertips and Ansley reached out and grabbed my arm.

"What are you doing? What if someone is still in there?" Ansley asked.

"Well let's go find out." I stepped over the threshold and into Brooke's house. "Hello? Brooke, are you home?" I called out.

"Come on, Mackenzie. Let's just go back to the car and call the cops." Ansley was standing on the front porch, chewing the nail off her thumb.

"We don't even know if anything has happened. Come on." I motioned for her to follow me.

She obeyed, but stuck close behind. I hadn't seen this side of her. She seemed like a frightened child. As soon as we reached the back living room, *I* felt like a frightened child.

I saw the blood before Ansley and turned to cover her mouth to muffle her screams. The ceiling, the walls, the carpet, all looked as though someone had thrown dark red paint throughout the room. I handed Ansley my cell phone.

"Go outside and call the police," I instructed.

She ran out to the front porch and dialed the number. My eyes scanned the room until I spotted Brooke's body. That's all it was though, a body. Every limb had been removed and she had been decapitated. This poor woman had been butchered. Her legs had been chopped off at the hips. Her arms were severed at the shoulders. There were no signs of the removed parts and a blood pool had formed around the torso.

I could hear Ansley out on the front porch freaking out over the phone with the emergency operator. Her high-pitched squeals echoed through the house.

I noticed a blood trail at my feet. I followed the drops, careful not to smear any evidence. The trail led to an exquisite china cabinet on the back wall of the dining room. I crouched down to look closely at the crimson circles. They seemed to lead directly behind the cabinet.

"Mackenzie, the police are on their way. The nine-one-one operator said to wait outside," Ansley shouted from the front of the house.

"Okay, I'm coming," I said so softly I knew she didn't hear me.

I figured the police could uncover more than I could, seeing as they were trained professionals, I decided to leave the exploration to them. I turned and slowly started toward the front door. I kept my head turned back and my eyes on the sideboard. I just knew that had to be a doorway to somewhere.

As I joined Ansley on the front porch, it wasn't long before we heard sirens. As the police cars - about five of them - pulled up to the curb, neighbors within ten houses each way came out into the street to find out what all the commotion was.

The first officer on the scene immediately approached us. "Stay here. Sit down and an officer will be with you shortly to take your statements," he insisted referring to the lounge set-up off to the side on the porch.

The set-up was three wicker chairs and a wicker type sofa circling a wicker coffee table with a glass top. We each chose a chair and watched as uniform after uniform entered and exited the house.

One female officer walked in calmly, but ran out in a hurry and vomited her breakfast all over a beautifully blooming rose bush. When she stood back upright, a small chunk of egg, or what I thought was egg, stuck to the corner of her mouth.

"Stay here," I told Ansley.

"Where are you going?" She asked as I headed toward the door.

"I'm going inside. I can't take this waiting any more." I stepped into the house, acting as though I was supposed to be there and headed straight for the china cabinet in the dining room.

All the officers and a couple of homicide detectives were standing in the living room. None of them even noticed when I walked by. I stepped up to the cabinet and gently pulled on the left side trying to open it like a door. It made a loud cracking sound as it pulled away from the wall. I stopped and waited thinking one of the officers heard and they were going to come rushing in any second.

When no one came, I continued. Once it was opened completely I was staring at a staircase. The wooden steps led up to an attic type bedroom. It wasn't very big - maybe about fifteen feet by fifteen feet. There was a twin-sized bed tucked away in one corner. The walls were covered with newspaper articles about 'The Butcher' and pictures of women. Lots and lots of women. They were all alive and living their every day lives. This suggested Malachi had followed these women for quite a while.

The set-up of the room insinuated two separate scenarios. One, Brooke had been harboring a fugitive, or two, Malachi had been staying here without her knowledge, then ambushed her after coming home and killed her for talking to the police.

He must have thought she would tell them about his room or out him in some way. There must have been a reason why he would have killed her. Of course it was only speculation at the time due to the evidence presented, it all pointed right at Malachi.

As I began counting how many potential victims he had, I saw photos of Ansley and me. I now felt as though I *could* trust the one person I connected with most. By the time I counted the last woman on the wall, I realized there were more victims than the police knew about.

I headed back down the stairs remembering to look for the blood trail. There wasn't any blood on the stairs or even in the room. The droplets started at the bottom of the stairs. He must have opened the cabinet from the inside and began the murder there.

I left the door open so the police would see it. I figured due to the gruesomeness of the scene, they could use a little help. I went back outside and sat back down on the chair next to Ansley.

I reached over and grabbed her hand. Luckily, she didn't ask any questions. I wasn't ready to talk about what I had just seen.

Finally, Agent Daria and Detective Rage pulled up. After they exited the vehicle, they first spoke to the officers that where considered crowd control, then sauntered in our direction. We stood up and both started talking at the same time.

"Hold on a minute." Rage put his hands up and we both stopped. "Now, one at a time, please."

I went first. "There is a secret room hidden in the back wall of the dining room. There are newspaper clippings of each murdered woman found. There are also pictures of more women then you know about that could possibly be potential victims. There is a blood trail from the bottom of the stairs that leads to the living room where her torso is." I also explained to them the two scenarios of the room. By the time I had finished, the three of them were standing in front of me with their eyes and mouths wide open.

"Did you tell the police about the room you found?" Rage asked.

"I just left the door open and figured they would find it." I shrugged my shoulders.

"Let's go." Rage led us into the house.

Two feet in the doorway, a uniformed officer stopped us. I leaned over and told Rage I was able to get in unnoticed before and didn't understand why we were being stopped now.

Rage and Daria showed their credentials and he let us in.

"They may have found the room," Rage informed me.

We headed straight back toward the hidden room. The police were swarming the area. Rage told Ansley and me to stay put while he and Daria headed up.

There was no way I was just going to stand and wait. I grabbed Ansley's arm and headed toward the front of the house to the main staircase. The steps went up six, made a ninety-degree angle turn then went up seven more. At the top of the stairs was a loft set up as an office. To the right was a small guest bedroom.

Ansley stuck close behind me as we headed toward the spare room. It was like walking through a haunted house attraction with someone who just wanted the next doorway to be the way out. I stopped frozen in the entry.

A leg was hanging, by the toes, from the ceiling directly over the bed. The comforter was pulled military style tight, a quarter could have bounced. A scarlet pool rested in the center of the cover where the limb had dripped. Muscle and tendons hung down from where the leg had been severed.

I quickly ushered Ansley out of the room and to the other side of the loft where another spare bedroom was placed. I told Ansley to sit in the loft and wait for me to inspect the other room.

The second room had an arm hanging by its fingers from the ceiling. This room had a treadmill and some free weights neatly organized. The blood from the arm was everywhere in the room. It appeared as though the limb had been swung around and created a splatter painted effect on the walls, ceiling and floor. The only difference in the pattern was the puddle on the floor it had left directly below the spot where it hung.

I moved on to the master suite located next to the exercise room. Brooke's head was strung up by her hair directly over one pillow of the king size bed. Her eyes were open wide with fright. Her face had been slashed numerous times. Her trachea was still intact and hung down as though he took time and carefully removed her head so she could keep her windpipe. More strips of muscle and tendons hung down from the site of decapitation.

I decided not to go into the bathroom. Tears were streaming down my face. I motioned for Ansley to follow me downstairs. On the way over, she peeked into the master suite and screamed at the top of her voice. The high-pitched squeal had every single police officer, detective and agent running full sprint up the stairs at us.

I backed Ansley into a corner of the loft. Rage immediately took us both downstairs once there was an opening and all the police officers had split off into each room.

"The two of you need to get back into the car and go home. More police will be showing up soon and the two of you would just be in the way. Please just go," Rage said once we were back outside on the front porch.

"He brought me another package. This time he rang the doorbell at Jasper's house," I told him.

"Did you see him?"

"No. Charlotte, Jillian, Jasper and I were sitting on the back patio when the doorbell rang. Jasper is the one who got up to answer the door, but by the time he got there, the only thing he found was the box. He could have heard us talking on the patio about me coming here to talk to Brooke and decided he would beat us here. He could have been in that upstairs room when we were here the other day and felt as though she would incriminate him in some way and decided to eliminate her before she could reveal where he was living."

"Make sure that box makes it to the station." Rage pointed his finger at me like a parent would to a child.

"Don't worry. Jasper did that this morning while I was on my way here," I said.

"Do you know who he dropped it off with? I've been at the station since five a.m. and he hadn't been there. Or at least hadn't been when I left at one this afternoon to be here. It's going to be dark soon. Go on home and make sure I get that box tomorrow." Rage went back into the house.

Thirty

Driving home, mostly in silence, thinking about the horror I had just witnessed, about twenty miles from her house, Ansley broke the taciturnity.

"Do you own a gun?" She blurted.

"Do I own a what?" I was shocked at the question.

"A gun. Do you own a gun?" She said again.

"No, I don't. They are dangerous and someone could really be hurt."

"I think you should have one for protection. I actually have the perfect home defense weapon for you."

"Home defense? What would I do with it? I have never held a gun, let alone shot one before. I wouldn't even know how to use it." I was shocked that she could talk about a dangerous weapon so nonchalantly.

"I can show you. It really isn't that difficult. I have been practicing with Gabrielle since I recovered so if I absolutely had to I would know how to defend myself."

"Yourself and your child. I don't have any children to protect. I shouldn't have to use a gun to protect *myself;* Jasper should be the one to use a gun to protect the house and me. I don't like guns." I shuddered just thinking about it.

"Mackenzie, we are strong independent women. We should be able to defend ourselves. We shouldn't have to depend on a man to save us from danger." Ansley practically scolded me for being dependant on Jasper.

I pulled up to her house and she told me to come inside with her. She took me through the house and out the back to a storage shed. She opened the door and pulled out a shotgun.

"No way. I don't even know how to use it," I told her. "I thought you were talking about a hand gun or something small. That's huge. What is it?"

"This is a Remington eight seventy pump action 12 gauge shot gun. It's not hard to shoot. I'll show you." She reached into the shed and brought out a box of buckshot. She pulled a shotgun shell out of the box, loaded it into the magazine tube, pulled back on the pump, which popped it into the chamber, aimed it at a tree and pulled the trigger.

BANG!

The shot rang out and I flinched. Hundreds of pellets shot out of the shell and ricocheted off the other trees around it. I actually smiled when I saw bark fly from the trunks.

"See how easy that was? I'm telling you, it is actually empowering. It will make you feel self-sufficient." Ansley pulled back the pump action and the spent shell casing popped out and fell to the ground.

"Can I try?" I asked. I wondered how it would make me feel. I wasn't sure if I would like it as much as she seemed to.

Pulling another shotgun shell from the box, loading it into the chamber, Ansley handed me the gun and instructed me how to use it. I placed the butt against my shoulder, aimed the end of the barrel at the same tree she did and pressed my finger against the trigger. Feeling powerful with the weapon in my hands, the recoil almost knocked me off my feet and I stumbled back a few steps.

Agreeing to take the gun, I handed it back to Ansley in order for her to place it into a case and equipping me with a box of shells, she helped me put the firearm into the trunk of my car.

"I'll come by tomorrow and take you to the place I called home until he took me," Ansley said. "Let's call it a therapeutic session of repetition."

"Call it whatever you want. If you think it could help in any way, I can show you my house where he took me from too. If I can help you get over your fear, then you can help me get over mine."

"I am so tired of looking over my shoulder wondering if he is following me. I'm tired of hiding out in the woods. I want to be able to live my life free from fear."

"I know how you feel. I want out of the prison I have created in my head due to the fear of him actually completing my murder and getting his way."

"He has lived free long enough. We need to figure a way to help the police capture him so he cannot do this to another woman," Ansley said.

"How can we help? You plan on luring him somewhere and having the police standing by to come get him when he shows up?" I asked.

"We could you know. See if there was a way to get him to show up at your house, have the cops hiding somewhere to apprehend him when he gets there. Otherwise we can try to eliminate him ourselves with the gun."

"Ansley, I am not a killer. In no way am I going to stoop to his level, nor am I going to give him an easy way out. He is going to suffer for what he has done to us and many others. I want to make sure he rots in prison for the rest of his life." I told her.

"Your right, what am I thinking? I should really be thinking about Matthew. Let's just focus on our own recovery."

It was a new side of Ansley I had never seen before. I just brushed it off as grief.

Thirty-one

The next morning when I was showering before Ansley came over, I smiled as I lowered my body onto the shower bench Jasper had set up for me. He had it installed so I could shower closer to the water rather than sitting in the tub.

Once out of the shower, I must have changed my clothes about fifteen times trying to find something to wear. As soon as I chose the perfect outfit, I was ready to sit down and talk to Ansley about our future life long friendship. All that morning I didn't once think about the psycho killer out to get me.

I sat on the sofa reading a book, waiting. I peeked out the window a few times with anticipation. When Ansley finally arrived, I felt like a twelve year old having a friend come over to spend the night. I was so excited.

I opened the door and greeted her with a hug. "Hey Ansley. Did you have trouble finding the place?" I said, acting as though I wasn't waiting all morning for her to arrive.

"No problem finding the house. I was having a problem leaving. Matthew did not want me to go. Every time I try to leave the house, he always tells me I can't go because something bad is going to happen. It is so cute how over protective he has become since I explained to him how mama got her plastic leg." She giggled and followed me to the dining room.

Bringing out coffee and freshly baked blueberry muffins, I poured each of us a cup of Joe and offered a pastry to Ansley as I gathered my thoughts and took a deep breath.

"I have an idea I would like to run by you. What would you say to us teaming up to help victims of rape and amputees? I figure we can help amputees get over their fear of a new lifestyle. We can help the rape victims get on with their lives and understand the importance of pressing charges against the person who violated them if they hadn't already." I smiled hoping she would agree with me. I knew I was babbling I just hoped she didn't notice.

"I don't know, Mackenzie. I think I would rather just move on with my life and not relive that trauma everyday through other people," she said. "After they catch this son of a bitch, I want to get Matthew and return to a normal life. I am a licensed therapist and would like to go back to my career. I'm sorry, Mackenzie, but for now I am going to have to say no." She took a sip of her coffee and looked down at the table.

"No problem. I wouldn't ask you to do anything that makes you feel uncomfortable."

We finished our coffee and muffins then climbed into my car.

"Four years ago I felt like I had my life together. I was a successful therapist living in a high-rise apartment building downtown. Until that night, I felt like a professional businesswoman. An eligible bachelorette." Ansley began her story on the ride to her former apartment.

I parked in the parking garage and looked over at Ansley. She had a terrified expression on her face.

"Are you okay? We can leave at anytime." I said and rubbed her arm.

"No, I'm fine. I have to do this." She placed her hand on mine. "A healthy way of dealing with tragedy, a person must realize that though life has changed it is still worth living. Family support and therapy through reliving the life changing experience can help someone navigate the world toward a new life."

We climbed out of the vehicle and headed for the front doors. We walked right up to the manager's desk. When he spotted us approaching, he came out from behind his little room.

"This is the same guy who ran this place when I lived here. I had called him a month and a half after I recovered to explain what happened and that I would not be returning. He had my stuff professionally packed and delivered to Gabrielle's home," she whispered as he walked up to us.

"I thought I would never see you again," he said as he embraced her.

"Mr. Tinsley, this is Mackenzie Leigh. She is also a survivor," Ansley introduced.

"Nice to meet you sir," I said as I shook his hand.

"The pleasure is all mine," he said as he pressed his lips against my knuckles.

"We are trying a therapeutic approach to getting over the trauma of being mutilated and violated. By any chance is there any way we could possibly get into my old apartment?" Ansley asked.

"As a matter of fact that unit is vacant for the next couple of weeks. Let me get the keys for you." He went back into his little office area, which was practically an open room with three walls and a desk blocking the large opening in the front. There was just enough room between one side of the desk and one wall for him to get in and out.

He reappeared in front of us with a set of keys. "Same floor, same unit."

"Thank you Mr. Tinsley. I really appreciate this."

We started down the hallway to the right and headed toward the elevators at the end of the hall on the back wall. Ansley pressed the call button between the two possible elevators and the up arrow lit up. As we waited, she took me to that day.

"I remember coming home from work. I made small talk with Mr. Tinsley. I walked over here and waited. My phone rang. It was a patient. I can't tell you what it was about, but I do remember still being on the phone when I got up to my apartment."

The elevator tone notified us it had arrived. We stepped through the door. Ansley pressed the button for the eighth floor and the luminescent circle around the number lit up.

We rode the elevator up in silence. When it stopped on the eighth floor, the doors separated and Ansley hesitated. I pressed my hand up against the open door to keep the elevator from closing. I turned to look back at a frightened young woman. She didn't look like the same person who entered the elevator down in the lobby.

"Ansley, are you okay?" I asked. "Remember we can stop and go home at any time. All you have to do is say so."

She shook her head and stepped forward. "I have to do this."

She took a deep breath and continued, "I was on the phone explaining to my patient that I would be in the office at eight the next morning. Oh my goodness. I never made it. I hope she's okay. I need to find out what happened to her." She stepped up to the door and hesitated. Turning back to look at me, she said, "I'm going to have to talk to my assistant and find out what happened to my patient."

She had the keys in her hand, but she seemed to be somewhere else. I touched her shoulder and she jumped.

Out of defense, she knocked my hand away and grabbed my wrist.

"Ansley, are you *sure* your okay?" I asked placing my other hand on top of her hand she had used to grip my arm.

She seemed to snap back to reality and released me. "I'm so sorry Mackenzie. I guess I'm just a little on edge. This is still nerve racking."

"Thanks for the comforting words of encouragement. I can only imagine how I am going to feel seeing as I was attacked *twice* at my house." I said sarcastically, trying to lighten the mood and chuckled.

Faking a smile, Ansley inserted the key into the lock and opened the door. She flipped the light switch by the door, which lit up a sort of hallway that started with the foyer, a coat closet to the left and led into a moderately sized living room. Without any furniture, I couldn't tell how large it could still be when lived in.

Ansley hung back in the foyer/hallway just before the living room. "I came in and sat on the sofa for a few moments going over some transcripts my secretary had typed up from a few recorded sessions with the patient I had just got off the phone with."

She ran her fingers along the wall all the way around the living room. She stopped at the opening of the eat in kitchen. "I got up and headed to the kitchen for a yogurt." She went through the motions. Opening the refrigerator, she mimed reaching in and taking something out. She walked over to a drawer and pretended to grab a spoon.

She went over to the window and peered out. "I stood here until the yogurt container was empty. I headed over to the sink, dropped in the spoon, threw out the container. I headed into the bathroom to wash my face."

She opened a door on the back wall between the eating area and the kitchen area. She stood in the doorway breathing slowly and deeply. In through the nose and out through the mouth. I could almost hear her actually whisper those words.

After a few moments, she stepped into another small hallway. She touched the doorknob on the door to the right. Changing her mind, she turned to the door to her left, opened it. She didn't go inside, but stepped back in order for me to peek into the bathroom.

"I washed all the makeup off my face, pulled my hair up into a bun then turned to the closet to change into my night clothes." She turned to the door she had started to open first. She turned the knob and opened the door to a large walk in closet. Ansley was crying.

"As soon as I opened this door, there was an outfit I had never seen before hanging right here where my robe usually was." She pointed at a hook affixed to the inside of the door. "I said out loud, 'where did this come from?' As soon as the words left my mouth, he was behind me. His arm was clutched around my waist. He gave me instructions to get it and bring it into the bedroom. I did as I was told. He released me once I laid the clothing down on the bed." She took a few deep breaths then led me down the hallway, which was only a couple more feet, into the bedroom.

"Do you need to stop? Oh Ansley, your shaking," I said when I wrapped my arm around her shoulders. "Let's take a break. We can go out into the hallway and just breathe for a little while."

She pushed me away. "I'm fine. I'm almost done. Where was I?" She brushed the tears from her cheeks. "Right, he let me loose then instructed me on how he wanted me to put on the clothes." Her voice was soft, tears where streaming down her face and she stared at the blank white wall. "He forced me to get naked before I put on the clothes. I felt so violated."

In a quick motion, she turned to look at me, grabbed me by the shoulders. As she cried and practically yelled in my face, she shook me. "What did I do wrong? I did everything he asked, the way he asked. Why did he still take me? Why did he do this to me? Why did he do this to so many women?" She let me go and plopped down onto the floor weeping uncontrollably.

Her breathing quickened. She had a waterfall of tears streaming down her face. I sat down in front of her and placed a hand on her knee.

Looking up at me, she pushed my hand off her, stood up and ran past me back through the apartment. I was in the process of reliving my own traumatic experience in my head and couldn't move as I was dazed and in my own world.

All of the questions she brought up, I had already wondered the answers to those same uncertainties. As soon as I heard the front door slam shut, I snapped out of my daze and ran after her.

Thirty-two

The elevator must have been waiting on the floor and the doors opened the second Ansley pressed the call button. She was nowhere in sight by the time I got there. I pressed the call button repeatedly waiting for it to come back. After about fifteen seconds, I decided I couldn't wait any longer and headed for the stairs. I ran down the eight flights taking them two steps at a time.

Holding my prosthetic out in front of me the best I could, using my thigh muscles, I grabbed the railing on both sides of me and crutched my way down placing my right foot down on every other step. Twice my foot slipped and I almost fell. Fortunately, I was able to catch myself each time.

Finally making it to the first floor, shoving open the stairwell door, I ran past Mr. Tinsley, who was standing in front of his desk with a dumbfounded look on his face. He must have seen Ansley run past because the look on his face appeared as though he wanted to ask me something.

I made it out of the building and found Ansley sitting next to my car. I walked up behind her and placed a hand on her shoulder. I noticed her eyes were red rimmed and her face stained with tears when she looked up at me.

"Why did he do this to us and all those other women? What did we do to deserve this?" Ansley's voice was low. I had to strain to hear her.

"We didn't do anything, honey. There is something wrong in *his* brain. Look, let's go get some coffee, we can go to a diner, sit and relax for a few moments to recompose ourselves." I helped her to her feet.

She nodded as I opened the car door for her. I went around the other side and slid in behind the wheel.

I decided to go to the café I frequented with Jillian and Charlotte and pulled into the parking lot. We headed inside and I led her over to the normal Wednesday lunch table even though it was Thursday. We ordered our coffee from Jean.

"This is the diner where I met Malachi. He was a manager up until recently, now that he has been exposed for the psycho he is and on the run from the feds," I explained to Ansley.

"That's pretty creepy. Why would you bring me here? What if he shows up?" She asked, scanning the place with her eyes.

"If he comes here, he will be immediately arrested. The FBI is watching the place. I thought maybe we could ask a few people here if they knew anything about him or where he came from. Maybe he told someone his story."

"Serial killers tend to keep to themselves and don't usually expose themselves to the others."

"Maybe he could have joked with someone who didn't take him seriously. He could have said something that no one thought was going to happen."

Jean brought our coffee over to the table and I asked her to talk to us for a moment. She sat down and joined us at the table.

"Jean, this is Ansley. She is also a victim of 'The Butcher'," I said.

"You mean Malachi," Jean said with a snarky tone.

"So you are aware of his secret identity. Did you ever suspect him of anything out of the ordinary?" I began my questioning.

"I never really suspected him of anything. He was quiet and kept to himself. The only time he ever spoke was when it had something to do with the diner."

"Do you know if he had any friends? Was there anyone here that he would have gone out with outside of work?"

"Please, there isn't one person here who that guy didn't give them the creeps. You can talk to everyone; they will all tell you the same thing. I have to get back to work. I'll see you later, Mackenzie. Nice meeting you, Ansley." Jean stood and walked away.

"Well that was just awkward," Ansley said.

"I don't know what is going on around here, but I want to know. I think we should talk to the other employees." I took a sip of my coffee.

"How about we veer back to the task at hand? When you were in the hospital recovering, who came to see you?" Ansley asked.

"Just my support system, Charlotte, Jillian and Jasper. The girls have been in my life for as long as I can remember. I was raised in foster homes since I was six and my mother abandoned me.

"Funny enough, Jasper was also someone I had met in the system. We had recently caught up with each other and began dating. The three of them are my only family."

"That's good for you that you have family. I only have Matthew and now Gabrielle and her family. Growing up in foster homes I had a horrible childhood. I was determined to work my ass off so when I had children I could take care of them even if a tragedy took me from them and still be able to give them everything I never had," She said.

"Let me know when you are ready to head out. I feel like the longer I wait the less likely I am going to want to do this." I took a deep breath.

"The coffee is helping calm me down. Let me finish this cup, then we can go," she said lifting the lip of the cup to her mouth.

She placed the cup down on the table and nodded her head. I paid for the coffee and Ansley left the tip. We got into the car and headed into my nightmare.

On the ride over to the house, I was the first to break the silence. "The night I was taken started out with Jillian, Charlotte, Jasper and I in jail." I went over the details leading up to the phone call I received from Charlotte.

"I'm sorry for freaking out back at the apartment. I guess I'm still a little shell shocked," Ansley said as I put the car in park on the driveway.

"It is not your fault. It is okay to freak out a little when something traumatic has happened to you." We got out of the car and headed for the front door.

I stood there, frozen, staring at the entryway, key in hand. The scenes of horror that had happened behind that door replayed in my head. I didn't know if I was ready to face my fear at that moment.

"We can wait if you need to," Ansley told me, placing her hand on my shoulder.

"I think I have waited long enough. No offence, honey, but I don't want it to be four years down the road before I can even step foot in this house. I used to share this house with Jillian and had some happy memories here. I want to get those memories of the house back, instead of having horrifying memories of what someone else did to me."

My hand was shaking as I slid the key into the lock. I opened the door and stood at the threshold. The years I lived in that house flashed, like clips from a movie, in my head. From the day I moved in all the way to the last time I was there.

My heart was pounding so hard I thought it would burst right through my chest. I took a deep breath to calm down and stepped into the foyer. I looked to my right into the living room and noticed the chair he had used to abort my babies was no longer a fixture in my home. I was relieved to know it was gone.

"I don't know if I'm ready to do this yet. I'm not comfortable reliving that day yet. Would you mind if I just gave you a tour of the house instead? It has only been nine months for me. If you are still affected after four years, I can only imagine how freaked out I might get," I requested.

"This is a really nice house. Compared to the house I have been living in over the past few years, this place is a mansion. Gabrielle is great, don't get me wrong, but the house is nothing like this," she said as we settled into the living room.

"Thank you. Jillian helped a lot with upgrades. When we first moved in, this place was a dump. We had the yellow linoleum swapped out for sand colored scratch resistant tile. The kitchen countertop was olive laminate which we replaced with brown and white marble granite. All of the cabinets were light mahogany. Jillian decided since we changed the counter darker, she thought the cherry cabinets would flow better.

"The walls were a boring white. The kitchen, unfortunately, was papered with ugly nineteen seventies brown and gold wallpaper that was covered with daisies. We painted it mocha and added a little backsplash to cover the ugly and the boring. The carpet was so matted down from years of high traffic; we replaced it with this plush vanilla with sprinkles Berber. We were planning to sell for three times the amount we paid," I told her.

"So you and Jillian bought this house together?" Ansley asked.

"We also lived here together until she got married. She was helping me pay the mortgage after I was attacked, up until a few months ago when my severance pay ran out and Jasper decided he would pay for everything on the house until we got married, then he would help sell it."

"I know you don't know me that well, but do you think it would be okay if I rented the house from you after the whole 'Butcher' ordeal is over? I need to get back out on my own. Matthew and I can live here; I will pay rent and all utilities." Ansley had a sort of pleading in her tone.

"I think that could be arranged." I stood and walked over to hug her.

"Also, if you're okay with it, you think we could stay here tonight?" Ansley bit down on her thumbnail the same way Jillian did when she was nervous.

"As a matter of fact, I still have some clothes here. I just need to get something out of the car first." I felt like I could make a new happy memory in a place where I only felt fear and sorrow.

She followed me out to my car. I opened the trunk and removed the shotgun. It was still locked in its case.

"You haven't taken it out of the car yet?" She asked.

"Jasper is at home to protect me. I was saving it for a time I might need it and now seems to be that time," I told her as I closed the back of the vehicle.

She shrugged her shoulders in agreement. We headed back into the house.

I called Jasper to inform him of our plan. "I'm having a hard time with this whole therapy thing. Ansley has decided that if we stay the night, it could possibly help me get over my fear of being home by myself," I told him.

"You don't live in that house anymore. You don't have to worry about that," Jasper said in a soothing tone.

"I know, honey, but I don't feel comfortable being alone in your house either. I love you and I will see you tomorrow."

"Are you sure this is such a good idea?"

"Yes, I promise I will be careful and I will call you if anything goes wrong." I made a kiss noise into the mouthpiece of the phone before hanging up.

At the same time I was on the phone with Jasper, Ansley contacted Gabrielle and explained she wasn't coming home. I only caught one side of the conversation. "I'm sure we will be fine...I understand that...It was my idea...I promise...Okay...I love him too...Tomorrow...I will call if...Don't worry...Love you too Gabrielle...Bye."

Once we were both off the phone, I picked up the shotgun case and headed up the stairs followed by Ansley. Beside the point that I was hauling an extra fifteen pounds, I was taking each step slowly. Once we made it to the landing, I stopped.

"We can stay downstairs if this is too hard. I can understand how upsetting this must be," Ansley said.

I shook my head as though to shake me into reality. "The bedroom is over here to the left," I said as I led the way and ignored Ansley's concern.

In one swift motion, like a wave crashing against a rock, I hoisted the gun up onto the bed. Ansley stood next to me as I opened each individual locking mechanism. I lifted the top up and over exposing the weapon.

I stared down at the Remington 12 gauge shot gun. The indentations pressed into the side walls of the case showed the gun was held firmly into place. I didn't know what to do with it then, but I figured I would when the time came.

"Lean it up in the corner. That way it will be easily accessed when we need it." Ansley smiled.

"*If* we need it. I hope it is more of an if than a when. I don't want to use it, but if I have to, I won't hesitate."

I lifted the gun up off the foam insulation and placed it where she suggested. Closing the case, I re-latched each individual lock and slid it under the bed. Inside my purse was a box of buckshot rounds. I pulled it out and set it on the nightstand. I felt prepared for any thing life was willing to throw at me.

I walked over and placed my hand on the door knob of the closet. I took a deep breath and pulled the door open quickly, first looking at the empty hook attached to the door. Relieved, I began rummaging through the left over clothing for a couple of night shirts.

Pulling two down from the hangers, placing them on the bed, I went over to the dresser and pulled out a couple pairs of night pants to match. Once we dressed for bed, we settled in for the night.

Thirty-three

As we lay in my old bed, I wasn't sure what to say at this point. Growing up as an orphan, I never had friends over to stay the night.

"So what usually happens at a slumber party?" I giggled, trying to have some type of fun.

"Pillow fight maybe," Ansley laughed.

Both of us sat up and grabbed our pillows. We swung the feather filled cushions and wacked each other on the arm. We fell back on the bed, giggling.

The sound of glass shattering downstairs halted our fun. Our mouths and bodies were still. More noise caused us to jump up off the bed. I gripped the shotgun in my right hand, dumped the five buckshot rounds out of the box and onto the bed. I loaded the rounds into the magazine tube, pulled back the pump action and cocked it, slipping one round into the chamber ready to fire.

Ansley and I headed downstairs to investigate the noise. We took each step slowly. At the bottom of the stairs, we stopped and listened. All was quiet again.

We tiptoed to the living room. A rock the size of a softball was resting in the center of the room.

Ansley hung back at the opening of the living room as I stepped up to the broken window. The screen had been sliced open and was lying outside in the bushes.

I turned and met back up with Ansley. We headed down the hall toward the kitchen. I pointed the barrel out in front of me ready to fire at any moment.

As we entered the kitchen, Ansley slid along the wall and stopped, leaning against the pantry door.

I continued past the kitchen to the dining room leaving her behind. I stopped at the table, turned to look at Ansley. She had stepped away from the door of the pantry. I knew she had leaned completely against the door, but it was cracked open a bit. I saw the shadow moving through the gap.

"Ansley, watch out!" I yelled.

Before she could react, the door swung open. Malachi jumped out, grabbed Ansley around her shoulders and held a large hunting knife to her throat. The moon light coming through the small window over the sink reflected on the blade. He gripped the white bone handle tightly in his right hand.

I held the gun aimed directly between his eyes. "Let her go Malachi. Your anger is focused at me. Let's finish this, just the two of us."

"My anger is focused at me you self centered ego maniacal bitch. Not everything is about you. You always have been pretty fucking selfish."

Ansley was crying, "Please let me go," repeatedly.

"Malachi, please. If you are angry with yourself then why are you doing this?" I asked in a soft, soothing tone continuing to aim the barrel of the shotgun at his face.

"Because women are the reason my parents are dead. My mother was a great woman. She was the one who always made time for me. We played soccer and board games. She always had a snack on the counter waiting for me when I got home from school.

"Three months after my tenth birthday, all of a sudden she didn't have time for me any more. My snack was always there, but she never was. I believe that is the time she began her affair. I still needed my mommy at that age. How could she just abandon me?" His face was drawn down. He genuinely looked sad.

"Malachi, I'm sorry that happened to you…" he cut me off before I could finish.

"Shut up bitch! It is my turn." He pressed the blade of the knife harder against Ansley's trachea. Blood seeped past the silver and trickled down her neck. "My father was always so strict. All the discipline I received was from my father. When I found their bodies, my father had explained to me in a letter why he had done what he had done." A single tear rolled down his cheek. That was the first sign of any kind of emotion, other than anger, I had seen from him.

"Is there anything I can do for you? I can help you get some therapy. Please, Malachi, don't do this," I pleaded.

"This is my therapy. Killing is my therapeutic way of getting over my parents death. Women don't appreciate the men in their lives and what that man does for them. I took care of you, both of you. I watched the two of you to keep you safe. Both of you betrayed me," he said, pressing the knife harder into Ansley's neck causing more blood to spill down onto the collar of her shirt.

"Please believe me, if I knew you were there, if I knew you were protecting me, I would have let you know how much I appreciated it." I tried to calm him down.

"No! You couldn't know. I wanted to see how loyal you could be to me. I talked to you on numerous occasions and never once did you show any interest. You never showed me any appreciation!" He stomped his left foot, then laughed. "Bet you wish you could do that."

"I'm done trying to negotiate with you," I said, irritated. "Let her go, Malachi."

Ansley continued to sob uncontrollably. I bit my lower lip to keep from screaming at him and giving him the satisfaction of knowing he was getting under my skin. I was still hoping that at some point he would let her go and I wouldn't have to pull the trigger.

"My life went to shit when my father found out about my mother's adultery. All those years of marriage thrown away for an affair. He cut her leg off to keep her from getting away as he questioned her. After she took her last breath, he felt so guilty he retrieved his .22 and killed himself. Women are cheats and liars. That is why they all must die."

With one smooth motion, the blade sliced open Ansley's neck. He dropped her body to the floor as she gasped for air. He lunged forward at me and I pulled the trigger.

Thirty-four

The top of Malachi's head exploded. It was as if a bomb had gone off in his skull. Blood, brain matter and skull fragments flew in every direction. The floor, walls and my clothes were splattered with the crimson liquid.

As soon as his body flopped forward onto the floor, I dropped the shotgun. I hurried over to Ansley grabbing a dishtowel off the counter as I knelt down next to her. I wrapped the towel around her neck to try to stop the bleeding.

Her breathing quickened as she gasped for air. "Relax honey. Just concentrate on staying alive. I need you, Ansley." I grabbed the cordless phone off the charger hanging on the wall and dialed nine-one-one.

"Nine-one-one, what is your emergency?" The operator asked.

"I need police and an ambulance right now," I said surprisingly calm.

"Alright ma'am, I need you to tell me what happened." She verified the address.

"My friend has been stabbed. She has lost a lot of blood and can barely breathe. Please, she needs an ambulance."

"Ma'am, do you know who stabbed her?"

"Yes, I shot him. That is what the police are for." My heart was pounding in my chest with panic.

I was afraid she was dying. No matter what I did, I knew there was no way I was going to save her.

"The ambulance is on its way. Can you stay on the line with me until they arrive?"

Before I could answer, I could hear the sirens. "I can hear them coming. Thank you for all your help." I hung up the phone and threw it down next to me.

I placed my hands over the towel. Blood was pooled around her from her shoulders to the top of her head. I was afraid to apply too much pressure in fear that I may cut off her air supply or crush her trachea.

She closed her eyes. "Don't die on me. You are not going to die. Open your eyes and look at me." Her eyes fluttered open as tears flooded from mine. "You are going to get through this. You are a strong woman," I encouraged.

Her eyes went wide and began blinking frequently as though she were letting me know she was still with me. When the ambulance arrived, two emergency technicians burst through the front door with a stretcher in tow.

"We're back here," I yelled when I heard the door slam against the wall.

They ran straight back to the kitchen. The stretcher was left at Ansley's feet. An oxygen mask was placed over her nose and mouth. The towel was removed from around her neck and replaced with sterile bandages. Gently they rolled her onto her side then back down onto a backboard. She was then lifted onto the stretcher and rushed out to the ambulance.

"Can I go with her?" I asked the EMT's.

"No ma'am, I'm sorry." The back doors to the ambulance were closed and I could no longer see Ansley.

I rushed to my car and followed the ambulance keeping my eyes glued to the back end. I phoned Jasper, Charlotte,

Jillian and even Gabrielle. All I told them was to meet me at the hospital as soon as they could.

The ambulance pulled up to the emergency entrance and I proceeded to the parking lot. I parked and ran up to the back of the ambulance just as two doctors in white coats and three nurses in blue scrubs came running out.

"Where are you taking her?" I asked, in which I was ignored.

"What do we have?" One doctor asked the emergency medical technicians.

"White female, throat slashed. She lost consciousness about three minutes ago. Substantial blood loss," the EMT replied.

"Please, tell me where you are taking her. I need to inform her family," I asked again, only this time forcing one of the doctors to talk to me.

"She is going to surgery to close up the gaping wound in her neck," he told me then pushed me aside.

The doctors and nurses took her straight back to surgery. I followed as far as they would let me, then stood there staring at two windowless doors. After a few moments, I meandered out to the waiting room.

Not long after I had sat down Charlotte, Jillian and Jasper walked in and joined me. "Did you happen to see Gabrielle when ya'll came in?" I asked as I hugged the three of them, simultaneously.

"No honey, I'm sorry. We didn't see her. What happened?" Jasper asked.

"It's Ansley," I began. "I couldn't save her. He was already in the house. I didn't know what else to do. Now she is in surgery and I don't know what is going on. No one has come out to keep me updated on her condition.

"I could go to jail. I killed a man. This is all my fault. I should have never let her in on the investigation. I should have never agreed to stay in that house." Tears were streaming down my face as though someone had turned on a faucet inside my head and it was over flowing out my eyes and nose.

"How do you think he found you?" Jasper asked.

"He has probably been watching the house and noticed the car in the driveway," I said. "Why isn't anyone telling us anything about her condition?"

"I'll go find someone who can tell us how she is doing," Jillian said before running off.

A moment later, Gabrielle came running in with Matthew on her hip. She set the boy down on one of the chairs, with a toy to play with and stepped the ten feet to where we were standing.

"What the hell happened? You had better have an explanation," Gabrielle accused.

I recounted the events for her. She was silent and lowered herself into one of the chairs. She stared at the floor breathing heavily. Her head shot up and she glared at me straight in the eye. The anger in her eyes was so heavy; I thought I saw the brown turn ruby.

"I didn't want any of this to happen. I tried to help her," I attempted.

"You did this to her. It is all your fault." Her cheeks were stained with tears.

"Now wait just a minute. Mackenzie tried to save her. She is in surgery right now. Jillian went to find someone to update us on her condition. Just calm down until we know more." Charlotte stood between us as though she were ready to fight if need be.

Gabrielle's gaze fell back to the floor. Finally, Jillian returned with a man in a white coat. He looked confused as she practically dragged him by his laboratory coat.

"How's Ansley? Is she going to be okay?" Gabrielle questioned.

"Were they able to stop the bleeding? Is she going to be able to speak again?" I asked.

"I'm sorry everyone. Mrs. Kirkland is still in surgery. Once they are finished the surgeon will come out and inform you of her condition. Please, just wait a few more minutes. I'm sure it won't be much longer." He turned and walked away.

We had to wait another excruciating ninety minutes before the surgeon came out. Gabrielle picked up Matthew and we all surrounded the doctor. He had blood on his collar and sleeves. A grave expression filled his face as he began.

Thirty-five

Six months after 'The Ansley Kirkland Center for Recovery' was opened, I was preparing everyone for my month long honeymoon. The center was up and running a short three months after Ansley's death and I was determined to keep things running smoothly even though I wasn't going to be there.

Jasper, Charlotte, Jillian and even Gabrielle were a few of the staff. We were lucky enough though to acquire Gabrielle's brother Marco, the prosthetic specialist. Everything was working out wonderfully. The center was housed in a five-story Victorian style mansion with approximately forty bedrooms. The rooms were large enough that we were able to accommodate between two to three people per room.

The first floor was set up beautifully. Right through the front door was a large foyer that opened into the reception area. To the right was the amputee group therapy room and to the left was the rape group therapy room. Directly above the reception desk, on the wall, hung a painting of Ansley.

The second floor housed children. The third floor housed the rape victims who weren't ready to go home. The fourth and fifth floors were the amputee victims separated by floor, male and female.

Gabrielle and Matthew moved into my old house. It was Matthew's idea. He said because his mother died in that house her spirit would always be there. He talked about her all the time and said he could feel her in the house.

Gabrielle was extremely angry with me for a while after Ansley's passing. When I told her I was going to dedicate the center to Ansley, she wasn't so angry anymore. She actually wanted to help.

Once the police took over her property to search for other bodies, Gabrielle was confined to her home. She decided she was going to move when the fourth body was unearthed. Matthew made the suggestion to her, she reluctantly made the suggestion to me and within a week she was completely moved into my old house.

After the police had scoured the entire property with the cadaver dogs and exhumed three dozen bodies – all of the victims were inside the same type of storage box both Ansley and I were found in. Some of the women were small enough for him to latch the lid. Those that were just a little taller and didn't quite fit the lid was just placed on top before he covered them with dirt.

Gabrielle was never going back and was determined to give Matthew a good life. She wanted to give him the life his mother had planned for him. Luckily, he was a sweet kid and had a lot of compassion for others.

He was a huge help with the children. Twenty five percent of them were staying with us due to the loss of a parent. He used a small loft area on the second floor to sit and talk to the children who have lost a parent. He had his own little therapy group. He was like a four-year-old therapist. It was amazing how mature he was for his age.

I was head of all group sessions. In my office, I was informing Gabrielle of the progress of our patients so she could oversee the groups while I was gone.

"Charlie and Dylan are leaving this weekend. Their grandparents are coming to pick them up. All the information along with photos of the grandparents is at the reception desk with Jillian. Charlotte has the files you are going to need for the rape group therapy sessions. Marco has agreed to assist with the amputee group therapy.

"There are four children being admitted next week." I pulled out a file with a list of their names and why they were going to be there.

"Three out of the four are coming due to loss of a parent. Johnny Grey is twelve years old. He will only be here until the investigation of the fire that killed his parents is completed. He is being investigated only because he was able to get out before the house was engulfed in flames. If he is cleared, he will go to live with his aunt and uncle. If they determine he is the one who set the fire, he will be admitted to a psychiatric hospital." I actually felt sorry for the boy.

"Is he going to be on watch? If he set the fire to his house, he could potentially set fire to the center." Gabrielle asked.

"Well, he will be staying with Charlotte in my room while we are gone. She is going to try and understand what happened. She is going to have her hands full with him though. He hasn't spoken a word since the fire."

"That is so sad. I hope she is able to gain his trust enough to get him to tell her what happened. Who else is coming?"

"Simone Feeney lost her father a year ago in Iraq. Three days ago, during a home invasion, she was knocked on conscience and her mother was raped. Susan will be here too. She is suffering from post traumatic stress disorder and needs help taking care of Simone."

"That poor child. Not only has she lost her father, but in a sense, she has also lost her mother," Gabrielle commented.

"That's not all. Aiden Warner lost his mother when he was two and she walked out on him and his father. His father was on his way to pick Aiden up from school a couple of days ago and was hit and killed when the other driver ran a red light." I had to stop a moment and take a deep breath.

"This is the saddest bunch of kids I think we have ever had at the center." A tear rolled down Gabrielle's cheek.

"There is still one more. Anthony Miller, fifteen years old, lost his arm in a skateboarding accident. He is being admitted later today. Apparently, he is also acting like a total teenager, attitude and all. His doctor from the hospital thinks he is not ready to go home. We are a sort of half way house for him." I handed the files over to Gabrielle and stood up.

"Don't worry, Mackenzie; everything will be taken care of." Gabrielle hugged me and we walked out together.

We headed out to the reception area where Jillian sat behind the desk. Gabrielle handed Jillian the files I had just gone over. "Please let me know when these guests arrive and also when Charlie and Dylan's grandparents get here. I would like to speak with them personally just like Mackenzie does."

"Jillian, while I am gone I want everything to go through Gabrielle as it would go through me, okay?"

"That's fine, I just don't understand why you couldn't put me or Charlotte in charge," Jillian said bitterly.

"Jilly, I need you to run the receptionist desk and Charlotte is in charge of the accounting department. Please understand that you all have very important jobs around here and I need each of you to continue doing those jobs. Gabrielle can help with new patients and explaining the meaning of the center," I rationalized.

Jillian shrugged and went back to her work. I walked through the rest of the center with Gabrielle. I introduced her to the patients. The rape victims were the only guests nervous about me leaving. I assured them I would be back and that Gabrielle would help them as much as she could.

I was excited to go to Europe for a month. Once I was certain everything would be okay, I went to the room Jasper and I lived in to pack. That in itself was a two-day job.

Over the last month, I had purchased a completely new wardrobe for the trip. I wasn't even taking any of my old clothes.

When Jasper handed me his credit card he said, 'a new wardrobe for a new life'. It was the best shopping spree I had ever been on. Of course, it was because I was spending someone else's money.

Luckily, Jasper was easy to pack. He gave me every pair of pants he owned with a shirt to match.

I had to pack at least three to four outfits for each day in order to dress according to mood. If my mood changed during the day, I would have to change my clothes. Jasper said that was what made me a woman.

He always knew the right thing to say. We were more in love as adults than we ever were as children.

Our wedding was all set to make me feel like a queen. We had rented a ballroom for the reception. My dress was Vera Wang as well as was the bridesmaid dresses. The colors were lilac, white and soft green.

I sat on the bed after I finished packing Jasper's three suitcases, staring at the seven I needed to pack for me. I laid down on my back glaring up at the ceiling remembering all the good things about Ansley.

I only knew her for a short time, but felt such a connection to her, I felt as though I had known her for a lifetime. I could still see her face in my mind.

I stood up and walked over to the window. I looked out into the front yard. The grass was a brilliant green. A landscaping crew had come in and put a fountain in the center of the garden.

Walking trails, about seven miles long, circled the fountain and lead a maze like trail throughout the yard. Each flower was strategically planted so not one of them had a flower of the same color next to it.

"Hey, Mackenzie," Charlotte's voice lingered in the doorway. "Girl, you better get to packing."

I turned to face her. "I was just admiring the view. What's up?"

"This envelope was mixed in with the mail. There is no return address nor does it say who it's for."

"Let me see it." I took the envelope from her and examined it.

The elegantly designed silver paper had me wondering if one of the guests decided to send a wedding card. I hesitated before opening it.

I pulled the adhesive apart and exposed a card the same color as the envelope. I pulled it out of its housing. On the front, in an eloquent script, was embossed 'Congratulations' in a sparkling white.

"Must be a wedding card from someone," Charlotte said as she peeked over my shoulder.

"Why wouldn't they want me to know who sent it though?" I wondered out loud.

"Maybe they signed it. Open it up."

I lifted the card open. On the inside was a message pasted of individual letters cut out from a magazine which read:

I've come back for You!

Forbidden Affair is the first novel by C. L. Conolly. She is in the process of completing three more and hopes to have finished five novels in the next three years. C. L. Conolly has been writing since she was six years old and has studied the sadistic minds of the most infamous serial killers in order to be able to write accurately. Happily married with one child, C. L. Conolly lives near Houston, Texas. Like her on Facebook.

www.ingramcontent.com/pod-product-compliance
Lightning Source LLC
Chambersburg PA
CBHW020417110726
47899CB00006B/2027